I REMEMBER

Acclaim for Julie Cannon's Fiction

Breaker's Passion is…"an exceptionally hot romance in an exceptionally romantic setting. …Cannon has become known for her well-drawn characters and well-written love scenes."—*Just About Write*

In *Power Play*…"Cannon gives her readers a high stakes game full of passion, humor, and incredible sex."—*Just About Write*

About *Heartland*…"There's nothing coy about the passion of these unalike dykes—it ignites at first encounter and never abates. …Cannon's well-constructed novel conveys more complexity of character and less overwrought melodrama than most stories in the crowded genre of lesbian-love-against-all-odds—a definite plus."—Richard Labonté, *Book Marks*

"Cannon has given her readers a novel rich in plot and rich in character development. Her vivid scenes touch our imaginations as her hot sex scenes touch us in many other areas. Uncharted Passage is a great read."—*Just About Write*

About *Just Business*…"Julie Cannon's novels just keep getting better and better! This is a delightful tale that completely engages the reader. It's a must read romance!"—*Just About Write*

Visit us at www.boldstrokesbooks.com

By the Author

I Remember

by
Julie Cannon

2013

I REMEMBER

ISBN 10: 1-60282-866-0
ISBN 13: 978-1-60282-866-7

This Trade Paperback Original Is Published By
Bold Strokes Books, Inc.
P.O. Box 249
Valley Falls, NY 12185

First Edition: April 2013

Credits

Editor: Shelley Thrasher
Production Design: Susan Ramundo
Cover Design By Sheri (graphicartist2020@hotmail.com)

Dedication

To Mom
I will always remember how you loved me

Chapter One

S he wished they would stop talking about it. Everyone had something to say: a comment, a question, or a request to see pictures. In the two days since she'd returned home she'd alternated between wanting to remember every minute of the last month and praying she'd forget it ever happened. Yeah, right. Like that would ever happen.

She was late. She hated people who were late to meetings. It was disrespectful. Like their time was more important than that of the other people who made the effort to actually be on time. As the president of Martin Engineering, Emery Barrett set the tone for these types of things. It was well known that she started her meetings on time, was always prepared, and ended promptly.

This morning, however, she was failing in everything. She had slept through her alarm, driven right by the gas station, and pulled into the parking lot on fumes. Her desk was piled high with things that needed her attention, and she hadn't even read the résumé of the woman she was interviewing in five minutes. No, check that—five minutes ago.

"Emery, you look wonderful."

"Your tan is fabulous."

"I love your new haircut."

"I am so jealous. I wish I could take a cruise anywhere, let alone three weeks to the Caribbean."

"I don't think I've ever seen you looking so rested and relaxed."

The well-meaning yet disconcerting comments from her employees continued as she hurried down the hall. At least they were from those brave enough to talk to her, let alone say something personal. She had been a royal bitch the past few months, and nothing she did pulled her out of her funk.

The plush carpet muffled any sound of her booted feet moving faster than they had in weeks. Yes, ladies and gentlemen, she thought as she returned their greetings. This is what a woman looks like after she's had sex, made love, and even fucked half a dozen times every day for exactly nineteen days. Take a good look because you'll never see it again, she wanted to say. Instead she simply offered polite thank-yous.

Anything other than that would have been totally out of character for Emery. But why stop now, she thought in that split second before she replied. She'd spent three weeks portraying a character she didn't even recognize. A different name, different look, no phone, no e-mail, no one needing something from her, wanting a piece of her.

But she had no choice. Actually she did, but the options were not in her favor. She was thoughtful, logical, and always studied both sides of the equation before making a decision. And the decision to leave her company, even if it was in the exceptionally good hands of her staff, to go on a cruise had been easy. It was the third "episode" that had scared the ever-living holy shit out of her.

The first she ignored, explaining the dizziness, complete lack of brainpower, and slightly slurred speech as stress and not remembering the last time she ate. That and the deadline she was facing to refinance ten million dollars of debt. She was a specialist in turning around companies on the verge of bankruptcy. Martin Engineering had hired her as their president three years ago to clean up the company's financial books and deal with a myriad of ethical violations related to securing government contracts. Federal auditors had Martin under the microscope, and Emery was on a tight timeline to turn it around. Any hint of scandal, or if two plus two didn't equal four every single time, and Martin Engineering would be history. Holy Christ, who wouldn't be a little frayed around the edges.

The second episode sent her to the doctor. The third to the emergency room, followed by three days in the cardiac wing of the local hospital hooked up to wires and machines measuring and monitoring everything going in and coming out of her body.

She was under doctors' orders to rest, and only because her best friend Julia's sister owned the cruise line had she managed to get a last-minute berth on the *Seafair*, a fifteen-passenger deck, twelve-hundred-foot-long, one-hundred-eight-foot-wide, class 1A1 passenger ship. She was one of two thousand passengers on the lesbian cruise and, along with a crew of thirteen hundred, spent twenty-one days cruising the southern Caribbean.

She had spoken with Dee Walker the first evening on the ship. On the second day they met for brunch and several games of billiards, and ended up after dinner in her stateroom. They never got out of bed on the third or the fourth day, and the remaining two weeks was much the same, with an occasional trip off the ship to sightsee or shop. For Emery it was by far the most exquisite sexual experience of her life.

She stopped just before the door to the conference room. She had to pull it together and get her head back in the game. She ran a multi-billion-dollar company, and she couldn't spend hours reminiscing about a beautiful, sleek woman with golden hair lying in her bed. She had a company to run, and the first thing on her agenda was to interview for the open strategy position on her staff.

The door was slightly ajar and she heard voices as she quickly read the top two lines on the thick paper.

DANA WORTHINGTON
CANDIDATE FOR VICE PRESIDENT CORPORATE STRATEGY

The headhunter Emery had hired had highly recommended Dana, and she had passed the rigorous set of interviews with the other members of the selection committee. Her qualifications were not in question, because if Ms. Worthington was seeing her now, the people Emery trusted completely had vetted her. Emery's role at this point was to see if she liked her, if they had chemistry and thought the same way about things, if she had the right fit and finish, and all of the other buzz phrases that determined if she was right to be included on Emery's tight-knit team.

She was particular about the makeup of her staff. She had handpicked all of them because the synergy among the members of her leadership team was critical. They were as fine-tuned as the jet engines Martin Engineering designed. She didn't want to upset that applecart, and this would be the topic of the first of several discussions she would have with Ms. Worthington.

Emery rapped on the door and pushed it open. Conversation stopped and three people stood as she entered the room.

"I apologize for being late. I have no excuse other than time just got away from me," she said to the two men and one woman politely standing around the mahogany table.

"No problem, Emery. I'm sure it's hard to get back into the swing of things," Jack Beecher, her vice president of human resources, stated to no one in particular. Phil Johnson, her CFO, nodded in agreement. Emery saw Jack turn to the woman and add, "Emery just got back from three weeks on a cruise. Dana, this is our president Emery Barrett. Emery, this is…"

Emery's world stopped. Her heart didn't beat, she didn't breathe. She couldn't move. This couldn't be happening. It was a cruel joke and she was the bad punch line. Never in a million years could she ever envision this scene. What had Humphrey Bogart said in *Casablanca*? "Of all the gin joints in all the towns in all the world, she walks into mine." Well, this just tops it off, she thought. Of all the open jobs in all the companies in the world, she walks into mine.

Dee Walker was Dana Worthington.

Chapter Two

This wasn't real. It couldn't be. EJ Connor was Emery Barrett? That was absurd. They had been together for three weeks, she'd said her name was EJ, and she'd never mentioned she was the president of the largest independent jet-engine-design company in the world.

Dana suddenly realized she was the one who was absurd. They had talked about everything from anarchists to the best zoo in the world but had somehow never shared what they did for a living. EJ/Emery had never asked and she hadn't volunteered. She too had given a false name when she first met EJ/Emery so that kettle can't call the pot black.

Dana recovered and extended her hand. "Ms. Barrett." Dana used the new name that went with the face that had hovered over hers so many times. She pushed the thought aside. "Dana Worthington. Thank you for meeting with me."

Emery hesitated for a second before stepping forward and acknowledging the greeting. A familiar jolt of electricity and desire surged through Dana's body when their hands touched. An identical look that Dana would never forget flashed in Emery's eyes, though she quickly masked it with professionalism.

"Likewise, and please call me Emery," said the voice that had whispered to her in the dark. "Everyone sit down. Again, I apologize for being late."

Dana had no idea what she said for the next ninety minutes. She forced herself to not look at Emery unless she directly asked her a question, and then she addressed her answer to the two men across the table from her as much as she could without being rude. She wasn't the least bit timid or shy and always looked people in the eyes when talking to them, but every time she glanced at Emery, a flashback of a minute or an hour or a night they had spent together clouded her brain.

She must have responded appropriately, because when the interview was over the men were shaking her hand so excitedly she thought they'd pull it right off. It was Dana's turn to hesitate when Emery extended her hand, preparing herself for the voltage she knew would come when their flesh met again. She wasn't wrong and could have sworn she heard Emery's quick intake of breath. Emery mumbled a polite good-bye before one of the men escorted her to the elevator.

Emery watched Dana walk away. This was by far the most surreal interview of her life. She had sat across the table from a woman she knew intimately and listened to her provide sharp, insightful answers to every question and scenario they threw at her. Emery had barely been able to concentrate as her eyes kept straying to the smooth neck she had nibbled on, the full, red lips she had feasted on, and the swell of the breasts she had caressed. When Dana had used her hands to accentuate a point, Emery had completely lost track of the conversation, remembering the first time those strong fingers slipped into her.

"Emery?"

Jack spoke beside her. "I'm sorry, Jack. What did you say?"

"Are you okay? You seem a little distracted."

That is the understatement of the universe, she thought. "No, I'm fine. I mean, yes, I'm fine." She corrected herself and stared at Jack. "What was your question again?"

"I asked what you thought of Dana?"

Holy crap, she thought. Just how am I supposed to answer that? Let's see, I can say that I think Miss Worthington is smart, intelligent, and quick-witted. I can also tell you that the Dana I know as Dee is witty, charming, funny, tender-hearted, intense, daring, passionate. She also eats like a horse, treats the wait staff with respect, and can be an absolute maniac in bed.

"Emery?" Jack's voice sounded more than a little concerned.

She pulled herself together. She was never anything other than in complete control in the office. Her thoughts never wandered and she focused intently on the here and now. However, in the two days since she left Dee/Dana at the dock in Ft. Lauderdale, she was constantly drawn back to the there and then.

"I think she's excellent. The selection committee did a good job finding her."

"Do you want to see her again?"

Do I ever. "Yes, make it lunch this time."

"Do you want it to be just the two of you, or do you want Phil and me along?"

Absolutely no one except me and Dee. "No, just the two of us will be fine. Sometime in the next week or so, if she can make it." Emery knew Jack would work out all the details.

She had to stop thinking of Dana as Dee. If Dana came to work here, and after this meeting it was a very big *if,* she would have to make sure she never called her Dee. That was another notch on the very weird post. Whoever would have thought this would happen? It was like something on the Lifetime Movie Network, except that it featured two women who had used aliases and kept their private lives private, yet had become extremely intimate. You couldn't make this shit up.

CHAPTER THREE

I t was who?"

"EJ, the woman I told you about on the ship. Her real name is Emery Barrett and she could be my next boss!" Dana kicked off her shoes and juggled her cell phone, briefcase, and suit jacket before tossing the jacket onto the back of the chair.

"Holy shit."

Lauren, Dana's best friend for her entire adult life, never minced words. They had met at Ogilvie and Mann when they were both summer interns, Lauren in the law department and Dana in marketing, and immediately hit it off. They had shared an apartment, hundreds of lunches, an occasional hangover, and talked at least twice a week. And they were still best friends ten years later.

"You took the words right out of my mouth," Dana replied, unzipping her skirt and kicking it into the basket to go to the laundry.

"Didn't you do any research on the company before the interview?"

Dana put the phone on speaker and unbuttoned her cuffs. "Of course I did. I know everything about Martin Engineering there is to know, and their president. There were several pictures of Emery Barrett, but she looked nothing like the woman I met on the boat. In the photo she had long dark hair and serious brown eyes. EJ had short, spiky hair with highlights through it, sparkling brown eyes, and the most radiant smile I've ever seen." And it was that smile that took her breath away every time.

Her blouse followed her skirt, and she covered her almost-naked body with a pair of old shorts and an Arizona Diamondbacks T-shirt. "I had absolutely no idea. It was the shock of my life."

"What did she do?"

"When she recognized me she had that same what-the-fuck look on her face. I stood there with my mouth hanging open for what felt like ten minutes."

"I can't even imagine what that was like."

"No shit," Dana replied, tugging on the refrigerator door. It squeaked open and she scanned the contents. She hadn't had a chance to restock after her three weeks away so the selection was pretty slim. Actually, she wanted a beer, but seeing it was only eleven thirty, even she thought it a bit too early. She settled for a can of Cherry Coke Zero. She popped the tab and took a long drink, hoping it would cool her off.

"We told you, you should have taken someone with you," Lauren said, referring to the conversation Dana had had with her friends the night before the cruise, over pizza and beer at their favorite Italian restaurant.

"There's no one I'm interested in enough to spend the weekend with," Dana had said, dipping the last chip in the salsa. "Let alone be trapped with in a tiny little room on a ship for three weeks. Besides, I'm sure I won't be the only single woman on board." She wasn't afraid of being bored. Her days were scheduled with both land and sea adventures in each port. She might be going alone but she would not be lonely.

"What about Tracey?" Sharon asked, referencing the woman Dana had taken to several of the group's date nights.

"She's too negative."

"Paula?" Dana had dated her earlier the year before.

"I could only take her in short time frames."

"Debbie?"

"She doesn't know when no means no," Dana said, remembering a very unpleasant ending to an otherwise pleasant evening.

"And before you name anybody else, I am perfectly capable of and actually prefer going on this trip alone." She held her hands up to stop Lauren from saying something. "I know you think I'm too particular and live in a dream world when it comes to finding the right woman, but I refuse to settle for anyone other than what I'm looking for." She wanted to become stupid, breathless, giddy, high-school tongue-tied, couldn't keep her hands off, completely and totally consumed by her desire for the woman she decided to share the rest of her life with.

"There is no such thing as the perfect woman," Maggie said, refilling Dana's empty mug with the remaining beer in the pitcher between them.

"I caught one," Lauren had said wistfully. Lauren and her partner Elliott had been together for several blissful years, and Lauren was expecting their first child in a few months.

Dana corrected her. "Don't you mean you let her catch *you*?"

"Well, there is that." Lauren rubbed her belly.

"I reiterate my claim," Maggie said decisively.

"Well, I think she exists. You can't tell me there isn't a woman out there who's confident without being arrogant, self-sufficient, independent, honest, and faithful, as well as cherishes her mother." There were several more attributes Dana wouldn't compromise on, but she didn't think she needed to bring them up.

"You don't even like your mother," Lauren said, a look of exasperation on her face.

Dana defended herself. "We're not talking about me."

Maggie piped up next. "You're talking about a woman that doesn't exist. No one's that perfect."

"I'm not looking for perfection, Maggie." But was she? Even though some of the women Dana dated had a few of her mandatory traits, some ended up being the exact opposite of what she had just defined. But she refused to believe there wasn't one woman who had it all. And she would remain single until she found her, even if it was years in the future.

"I like my own company and lately prefer it to those around me. Present company excluded, of course," she said quickly. "I'll be fine, have a great time, and will come back tanned and rested for my interview at Martin Engineering."

"Why are you going back to work so soon? You've got enough money to last you months. Take some time off, you deserve it. You work too hard. No wonder you can't find a woman."

"Maggie, that's not fair!" Dana was completely exasperated. They recycled this old topic of conversation at least once every few months. "I have no trouble finding *women*, as you call them. You just named three."

"And I could rattle off at least half a dozen more too, which is exactly my point," Maggie replied.

"And just how many women have you dated?" Dana knew the answer was far more than she'd just been accused of cycling through.

Maggie mimicked Dana's previous response. "We're not talking about me."

"And we're not talking about me anymore either," Dana said with finality.

❖

Less than twenty-four hours later Dee jumped at the blast of the ship's horn. She wasn't expecting it and had lost all track of her surroundings other than the feel of the warm breeze on her face. It had been far too long since she had gotten away from the rat race of her career, over-zealous friends trying to set her up with "the perfect woman," and her mother. The first was long overdue, the second well meaning if not a bit tiring, and the third just a plain old pain in the ass.

She was between jobs, having left her previous employer two weeks ago with a hefty severance check in her pocket. Brady and Black, a small boutique public-relations firm, had been acquired by one of the largest firms in the world, and within three weeks, she had packed her office possessions into two boxes and was saying good-bye to friends and co-workers she had spent thousands of hours with. Between her savings and the final check from Brady, she didn't have to worry about working for at least a year, and much longer if she sold the Microsoft stock her grandmother had left her.

Minnie, as her mother's mother preferred to be called, had been a woman far ahead of her time. She'd managed to save a dollar here and two dollars there for years and, unbeknownst to anyone, especially Dee's mother, had bought blocks of Intel and Microsoft stock when it was in the single digits. When she died at the ripe old age of ninety-two and her will was read, that was the first time anyone had any clue that Minnie was a multi-millionaire. She left it all to Dee, and her mother had just about blown a gasket. Deloris had been hounding her ever since.

This trip was Minnie's idea, in fact. Dee would talk to her grandmother for hours about everything. She was her sounding board for life, love, and work. Minnie taught her how to stand up for herself, give to those that didn't have, and cast her fishing line to the exact spot she was aiming at. When Dee said she wanted to go to college, her mother had scoffed but Minnie had supported her decision. When, at fourteen, Dee hesitantly confided in Minnie that she had "those funny feelings" for Karen Sharpe, Minnie hugged her and told her she loved her no matter what.

Deloris Worthington, on the other hand, loved easily and, based on the number of stepfathers Dee had, often carelessly. She was currently "between husbands," as Dee told her friends, positive her mother wouldn't disappoint her with yet another one soon. Her mother was more afraid of being alone than she was of being unhappy. Thankfully, Dee was nothing like her.

"So how do you think it went?" Lauren asked, pulling Dana's attention back to the present.

"You mean other than the obvious elephant in the room? I have no idea what they asked me or what I said, but I got the impression it was the right thing. They said they'd let me know in a few days what the next steps would be."

"I still don't understand why you want this job. Martin doesn't have a good reputation. If Emery Barrett doesn't pull this off you could go down with her."

"But she is turning it around. Sure, they ran into some trouble with the government and how they conducted business, but Emery has a fabulous reputation for taking a company on the brink of disaster and turning it into a huge moneymaker. Her reputation is phenomenal in this area, and the opportunity to be a part of this kind of transformation really interests me."

Dana had read everything possible on Emery, every article on her management style, and even went so far as to talk to several people who had been on her staff at other companies. Everything pointed to the fact that Emery was a dynamic, charismatic, shrewd, and very smart woman. One article in the *Harvard Business Review* went so far as to say her insight was akin to a crystal ball. She had an uncanny knack of knowing exactly when to take chances and when to play it safe.

"But if she doesn't succeed, you could go down with her," Lauren pointed out for the umpteenth time.

"She won't. She never has. Having me on the team increases her chance for success by ten times. I am exactly what she needs." Dana was nothing but confident in her capabilities.

"Is that what you told her?"

"Not exactly in those words but I got my point across. At least I think I did. I'm not sure what I said. It's all a little fuzzy after Emery walked into the room." The interview still felt a bit more than surreal even now, an hour after it.

"Do you think she'll hire you?"

That was the hundred-thousand-dollar question. Normally at this stage of the interview process Dana had a pretty good idea of the outcome. By the time she got to the CEO it was usually her job to lose. She'd never encountered this situation. She bet that the number of times it had happened to anyone in the world could probably be counted on one hand.

She and Lauren confirmed their lunch date for the next day, said their good-byes, and Dana took her Coke onto the patio. She settled into one of the high-backed chairs, her favorite spot on the deck. From here she could see the ocean through the trees and hear the birds chatting nearby.

She had debated with herself for months, trying to decide if she wanted to cut down some of the tall trees to enhance her view of the lake, but at the same time she didn't want to lose any of the thick, mature trees that had sold her on the property. In compromise she simply thinned out some of the dead wood and scrub and called it paradise.

She had bought the five acres three years ago and it was still a work in progress, as she often described it. The house was over a hundred years old, and even after new plumbing, wiring, a roof, and double-paned windows, it still needed work. Now that the house was foundationally sound she could begin on the inside. The plans to remodel the kitchen were on her desk in the study, along with the estimate from a local contractor. She had signed the contract, sent the first check, and was anxious to get started. He was scheduled to be on her back doorstep the day after tomorrow and, as he had stated on more than one occasion, "in only six short weeks" her kitchen would go from early 1970s—complete with the requisite olive-green appliances, practically non-existent laminate countertops, and a chipped cast-iron sink—to a high-efficiency gas stove and range, a Sub-Zero refrigerator/ freezer, and sixty square feet of granite countertop. She doubted it would be ready in six weeks but was prepared for it to take as long as necessary to be exactly as she wanted it.

Dana put her bare feet on the small table and settled in to think. She wanted this job. When she had first heard that Martin Engineering was looking for someone to help develop their long-term strategy she jumped at it, putting out feelers and inquiries until she connected with the search firm recruiting for the position. The fact that a female led Martin in a very male-dominated field also interested her.

Dana had endured an exhausting interview process even before she got to Emery. Between the two three-hour exploratory interviews with the search firm, the two-day executive assessment, and the five people at Martin she had spoken with, Dana felt like she had been poked, prodded, and examined to the nth degree. The final step was the interview this morning.

Talking with Emery simply reinforced her desire for this job. She wanted to work with a visionary leader, someone who had great ideas and wasn't afraid to take chances, and that person was Emery Barrett. But what about EJ Connor? What in the hell was she going to do with her memories of that person? What would her life be like if Emery offered her the job? Equally important, what would she do if she didn't?

CHAPTER FOUR

Somehow Emery got through the morning. Adam, her administrative assistant, ran her office like a tight ship and had everything completely organized for her return. A retired general's aide, Adam was a godsend on more than one occasion, and it was scary how he knew what Emery needed almost before she did. He could draft most of her correspondence and write her a thirty-minute speech with only a few key points that she provided. He had been her right hand, left hand, and everything in between for eight years. Some days she felt like she went wherever Adam told her whenever he told her it was time to go. And today was one of those days. Thank God, because she didn't know if she could have done anything by herself if she had to.

After the shock of the interview with Dana, Adam had kept her on schedule as she met with each of her department heads for a brief update of what had transpired during her absence. She was an absolute professional but couldn't keep her mind from drifting to the first day of the cruise.

The deck was crowded. Women of all ages, shapes, sizes, and colors jostled for position against the rail. Most were waving to familiar faces on the port, a few were kissing, some looked nervous, while others, like herself, were simply enjoying the warm late-afternoon sun on their face as the ship slowly moved through the crystal-clear water of the port of Ft. Lauderdale.

No one was sending her off on the twenty-one-day cruise to the southern Caribbean. She had insisted that Julia drop her off at the airport and continue on to work. Julia, her best friend since middle school, was a pediatrician with a bustling practice in Mission Bay, a suburb of San Diego, and, other than an acquaintance or two, EJ's only friend. Work kept her from taking the time to cultivate friendships, which was perfectly fine with her.

Her hair blew in her face and, irritated with it and just about everything in her life, she turned into the wind, effectively blowing it off her face. Squinting into the sun she saw another lone passenger standing at the front of the ship, or the bow, as it was known. EJ looked around for the woman's companion, wondering what she could be doing that was more important than being with her woman as the cruise began. She had read that entering and leaving the home port was one of the most memorable events of a cruise.

She watched the woman remove her cap and lift her face to the sky, as if worshiping the warmth. From her vantage point, EJ guessed she was probably shorter than her own five foot nine inches, and she thought ahead enough to put her long, blond hair in a ponytail. She was thin without being skinny, the muscles in her tanned, bare arms clearly defined without being too muscular. Whereas other women ogled breasts, legs, and butts, EJ admittedly was an arm girl. There was something dangerously sexy about a woman with muscles. Just by looking at her EJ could practically feel the confidence the woman exuded.

Maybe she was traveling alone, EJ thought, but then changed her mind. A woman who looked like that would have multiple choices of traveling companions. Maybe she was still unpacking and settling in. Maybe she was already seasick. There were a thousand maybes, and EJ knew only that if she were sharing the woman's cabin, she wouldn't be on the deck alone.

The blast of the ship's horn was loud and unexpected, and EJ saw the woman was as startled as she was. After the wretched noise stopped she watched her slowly walk around the deck stopping and chatting with several other passengers. From her vantage point EJ assumed she was making polite small talk. She'd seen it enough in the hundreds of obligatory social events that were a part of her job. The woman's conversations were brief, accompanied by courteous handshakes before she moved on.

The woman looked her way, their eyes meeting for a moment before she started a conversation with another couple. An unfamiliar sense of disappointment buzzed in EJ's chest, but a very familiar spark of interest flared somewhere else. This might just be the rest and relaxation the doctor *didn't* order.

Chapter Five

The restaurant Dana was looking for was just up the street on the left. She had been surprised when Jack, the head of human resources, called her and said that Emery wanted to meet for lunch. When Dana inquired if he or any other member of the Martin leadership team would be attending, her heart skipped when he told her that it would only be her and Emery. To say she was nervous was an understatement. She had gotten very little sleep the night before, her dreams filled with the first time she saw Emery.

Dee had been the last to be seated at her table, a stuck zipper making her arrive a few minutes late for dinner. She was looking forward to the opportunity to meet the women at her table tonight. The women she dined with were an interesting mix of young and old, and the conversation was lively and interesting. Dee felt someone's eyes on her throughout her meal, and when she looked around in an attempt to determine who it might be, she met the gaze of the woman sitting directly across from her a few tables away.

The woman with short, spiky hair looked to be in her mid-thirties, about the same age as Dee, and from what she could see was quite stunning in her black suit. Dee watched the interplay of the group at that table and guessed that none of the other women were traveling with her.

From thirty feet away Dee watched the woman's face transform from mildly curious to intensely interested. This trip might be more interesting than she'd anticipated, but then the redhead sitting next to the woman reached out and touched her, asserting her claim.

Dee choked down her disappointment with a fresh glass of cabernet. Something about the woman in black kept drawing Dee's attention, almost making her become rude to the others at her table. Even though she was on vacation and likely to experience things she had only dreamed about, she would never compromise her principles. And going after another woman's woman was number one on her unforgivable list.

Dana glanced at her watch. Even though she had spent ten minutes looking for a place to park, she was still a few minutes early. She took the opportunity to study Emery, who was already there and drummed her fingers on the top of the table. It was a nervous gesture she exhibited several times throughout their cruise, and Dana didn't think Emery was even aware of it.

Today she was wearing a dark-gray suit jacket over a plum-colored shirt opened at the collar. Dana knew the colors would bring out the flecks of red in her eyes—the flecks that flashed with desire. A glass of water sat half empty in front of Emery, the sweat dripping down the side reminding Dana of how Emery had looked walking out of the surf, water dripping off her firm, smooth skin, standing under the cascading water in the shower.

"For God's sake, Dana, pull it together. This is a business meeting. You've had dozens of them. This is just another one," she murmured softly. With the advent of the Bluetooth, nobody paid any attention to anyone that looked like they were talking to themselves. But as much as she tried to convince herself, this was not just another business lunch.

The hostess escorted her to Emery's table and Emery stood as she approached. "Thank you," Dana said to the woman just before Emery extended her hand.

"Ms. Worthington."

Emery's voice was as melodic and sexy as she remembered. Dana braced herself for the moment their hands touched. The same jolt of pleasure sizzled through her as it had every other time their flesh met.

The waiter took her drink order and Dana used the time to collect herself. Sitting across from Emery like this brought back far too many memories. She struggled to look her in the eye.

"This is…uh…awkward," Emery said.

"No," Dana said, her voice stronger than she felt. "Awkward was when you walked into that conference room the other day." Emery looked at her, then just as quickly glanced away.

"To say the least." Emery still didn't make eye contact. This Emery was far different from the woman she'd spent three weeks with. That woman was confident, sure of herself, and direct. This one seemed anything but.

"I suppose we should talk about it," Emery said.

"That depends."

Emery finally looked at her. "On?"

"On whether this is a personal or professional lunch."

Emery had no clue how to answer that question. She had lain awake most of the night trying to figure it out. She had always been able to separate business from pleasure, and working in such a male-dominated field had made it even easier. Rarely did she encounter a woman she was attracted to, and when she did she simply put the thoughts out of her head. Business was business and pleasure was pleasure. As simple as that.

In her adult life she had seen several instances where sex ruined a promising career and never understood how someone could let it happen. She was emotionally strong and believed that she always had control over her decisions. Things didn't "just happen." As far as she was concerned that was just an excuse.

At least her father hadn't made excuses. A successful auto executive, he had traveled more than he'd been at home, enabling him to have a series of affairs that blew up in his face when he met the wrong woman. When the dust had finally settled, Emery's happy childhood filled with security and love instantly turned into shame, humiliation, and endless teasing by her classmates. Her father lost his job and turned to drinking to solve his problems. Her mother, an emotionally frail woman to begin with, withdrew even further, allowing her husband to drink and her kids to go to bed hungry. Emery swore that she would never be as weak as her father or mother.

Emery answered honestly. "I'm not certain how to answer that."

"Which would you like it to be?"

She suddenly realized she was acting just like her father. She was weak, vacillating between what she wanted and what she needed to do. Her father had chosen the easy way, and she remembered that cold day in February when the house had no heat and she had to go to school wearing dirty clothes. That day had changed her life. From that point on she would not and did not allow her emotions to run her life. And look what she'd got for it. Almost killing herself under the stress of it all.

She sat up straighter and cleared her throat, willing her voice to be strong. "It doesn't matter what I'd *like*. I have a company to think about. Hundreds of millions of dollars are at stake in contracts, thousands of lives depend on me for their job, their livelihood, their future. Martin Engineering cannot be involved in another scandal. I've no doubt you've done your homework, Ms. Worthington, and you're well aware that we're on the watch list. Under a very large microscope, I might add. Any hint of a problem, a misplaced comma, or another of its executives caught with their pants down, so to speak, spells the end of Martin." Emery leaned forward and looked Dana straight in the eye. "And it will not happen on my watch."

The force of her words surprised even her. She had given the same speech dozens of times in the past three years. Whether it was at shareholder meetings, standing in front of employees at any of Martin's thirty-five locations around the world, or her own staff meetings, she would tolerate no misunderstanding.

"You are the best person for this job, Ms. Worthington, and I'd like to have you on my team. But if it gets out that we knew each other," Emery hesitated, searching for the right word, "socially, then your reputation is fucked, mine is screwed, and Martin Engineering is history."

Emery had thought very hard about what she would say to Dana today. If word got out that they had a prior relationship, Dana would forever be tainted with the label of sleeping with the boss to get a job.

"You look nothing like your picture."

Dana's statement caught her off guard. "What?"

"I researched Martin Engineering thoroughly and I didn't even recognize you."

"Yeah, well, that picture's a few years old. Amazing what a new haircut and a completely different setting can do," she said dryly.

"Where did EJ come from? EJ, the name you used on the ship."

Emery had been expecting this conversation, but she still felt completely unprepared. Then again, nothing about the last month was expected. She hadn't expected to collapse from exhaustion, be banished to a boat for three weeks, and hook up with a smart, charming, intelligent, sexy, passionate woman whom she ended up interviewing for a job. Just exactly when did her life go from everything in order to everything fucked up?

"My initials. Emery Jones. And Dee? Is that Dee spelled *D-E-E* or *D* for Dana?" Emery found herself asking.

"Either one. Walker is my mother's maiden name. Why the subterfuge?"

Emery didn't answer the question. "I don't remember either one of us asking any personal, probing questions."

Dana shook her head. "No, I don't suppose we did."

"So why the subterfuge?" Emery turned the question around.

"I don't know. It sounded like a good idea at the time. I wasn't looking to get involved with anyone, and keeping it light seemed the way to do it."

The waiter brought their lunch and Dana said, "You didn't answer my question."

Emery made a decision she hoped she didn't regret. "I was under doctor's orders to get away from the stress of my job and rest. What better way than to pretend to be someone completely different?"

The chatter of the women around the table hadn't stopped since EJ sat down. The seating chart for the seven-thirty dinner put her between a couple celebrating their twentieth anniversary and one of three other single women at the table alone. Next to the couple were newlyweds and to their left a pair of bleached blondes from Florida.

The room buzzed with the sound of excited voices meeting new friends. Jewelry glinted in the fluorescent lights, and everyone had heeded the notice that semi-formal dress was required. EJ felt comfortable in her Chanel silk suit, the deep-green shade adding color to her pale cheeks. She had stopped at the salon earlier this afternoon and instructed the stylist to cut it all off and give her a crisp, clean look." Three hours later her shoulder-length locks were gone and not a hair on her head was longer than an inch. That and the highlights made her look and feel ten years younger.

Tuxedo-clad waiters slipped silently between the forty-plus other tables, filling wine glasses and placing heavy plates on white linen tablecloths. The lighting was turned up, inviting conversation across the wide tables.

"EJ, where are you from?" Kim, one of the other single travelers at the table, asked. EJ had felt Kim zero in on her the minute she sat down. Kim was attractive, and any other time EJ would have taken her up on her obvious offer, but she was surprisingly not interested. Also her physician said she needed rest, and what Kim was silently proposing would be anything but.

"Las Vegas," EJ answered, naming her favorite city but not where she lived. When she booked this trip she'd decided to leave her entire life behind, and that included her name, hometown, and profession. Her middle name was Jones, and she would be less likely to slip if she kept her lies close to the truth.

"I love Las Vegas," Kim replied, her Southern drawl heavy. If EJ had been blind or somehow missed the glint of sexual adventure in her eyes, she couldn't miss Kim's warm hand lightly touching her forearm. "I always feel like a different person when I'm there. Absolutely nothing holding me," she hesitated for a moment and used the opportunity to lean into EJ, "except a sexy, exciting woman."

Kim's soft breast pressed against EJ's arm and she resisted the urge to shift and break the contact. She wasn't interested but didn't want to alienate her dinner partner. "Then I'm glad it's lived up to its reputation." One of the ladies to her left rescued EJ by engaging Kim in conversation. She sent her a silent thank-you for directing Kim's attention away from her—at least for a few minutes.

As the women talked, she surveyed the rest of the room. By reading body language and keeping in mind that this was their first night together, she suspected that similar get-acquainted conversations were happening at the other tables as well. Bored, she stopped her eyes from roaming when she spotted the woman who sat two tables away, directly facing her. It was the woman from the deck earlier this afternoon.

Her hair was down but pulled away from her face, highlighting her cheekbones and long neck. Her dress, what little EJ could see, was jade-green and sleeveless, accentuating those arms again. A clunky bracelet slid down her left arm as she tucked a strand of hair behind her ear. EJ's pulse kicked up at the simple gesture and increased tenfold when the stranger laughed at something the woman next to her said. Had the lighting in the room changed or was her smile actually that radiant?

For several minutes EJ couldn't take her eyes off the woman. She was animated, attentive, and impartially sociable. EJ wished she were seated at that table but changed her mind when she realized her current seating assignment gave her the unobstructed, undetected ability to simply watch her. Kim, however, had other ideas for her attention.

"EJ?"

"I'm sorry, what did you say?" EJ replied, shaking her head a bit when she realized someone had asked her a question.

"I asked what you did for a living?"

Kim was apparently more interested in her body and her bank account than her brain. "A little of this and a little of that," she said evasively.

Kim leaned close enough to whisper in her ear. "You'll have to tell me more about that later."

EJ pasted on a fake smile. She wasn't interested in telling her anything other than what she had to during polite conversation.

Dinner finally arrived and, as much as she tried to become interested in the conversation at her own table, her attention kept straying to the woman in green. The way she interacted with the others at her table made it apparent that she was definitely traveling alone.

On one occasion the woman caught EJ looking at her. She held her eyes the way women did when they were interested in what they saw, and EJ lost all sense of her surroundings. All sound ceased, no one moved, and nothing existed except the woman looking at her. She felt completely exposed as warmth spread through her body. Her mouth was dry and her hands trembled slightly.

The woman's eyes totally captured her. She couldn't look away even if she'd wanted to. She didn't believe in love at first sight and had often been immediately physically attracted to a woman, but she'd never experienced anything like this.

❖

EJ had intentionally followed the woman after she left the restaurant, wanting to speak with her. She had excused herself from the conversation around her when the woman rose and walked away from her table and out the door. In truth, she could barely speak for several seconds. The woman was stunningly beautiful in the green dress, perfectly cut to accentuate her height and draw attention to her face. A fashionable new length, the dress floated around the woman's mid-calf. As she walked, EJ glimpsed long legs before the back of the gown, cut low to display a healthy portion of the woman's tanned skin. The slight sway of feminine hips equally enticed EJ, who had to tell her mouth to shut.

The woman casually strolled across the deck and entered the mini-theater. EJ quickly read the notice that described the traveling troupe of the latest Broadway hit was performing three nights a week during the cruise. She wasn't a fan of live theater, but when the woman entered the auditorium she followed. She let the woman choose her seat and get settled before she approached. She couldn't have set up a more perfect first-meeting scenario.

"Is this seat taken?"

The bluest eyes EJ had ever seen looked up at her. They were bright, clear, and direct.

'No."

"Is *that* seat taken?" EJ asked, indicating the empty seat on the other side of the woman. The spark of understanding that flickered to life in the woman's eye when she answered the subtext of her question told EJ she'd heard the double meaning of her question. Her answer came slowly and EJ struggled not to fidget.

The woman was more beautiful up close, her skin flawless, her cheeks tinted with color. Her green eyes were sharp, intelligent, and unwavering.

"No."

"Then may I join you?" EJ hoped the answer this time was yes. Three no's in a row and she would definitely strike out.

The woman hesitated for several moments, as if weighing her options. EJ watched the questions cycle through her eyes. Uncharacteristically uncomfortable with the silence, she was about to excuse herself when the woman answered.

"What is the woman who was hanging all over you at dinner going to say?"

That certainly wasn't the answer EJ had expected, and she couldn't help but smile. So this woman had been watching her as much as EJ had been watching her. This woman wasn't only beautiful but definitely no-nonsense. Her heart beat a little faster. "I don't know. Probably something other than she pulled out all the stops to seduce me and didn't get anywhere."

Again the woman paused before answering. Her eyes darted back and forth at EJ's as if looking for a chink in her façade, a lie waiting to be uttered or fate to intervene. She certainly hoped it was the latter. On the occasions when someone had turned her down she had accepted the rejection without issue, but for the first time in a long time she really wanted her to say yes. She wanted *this woman* to say yes. Her heart jumped when the woman tilted her head and smiled at her.

"Please do."

Before EJ sat she extended her hand. For some odd reason she was surprised to see it wasn't shaking. "EJ Connor."

This time, without hesitating, the woman slipped her hand into hers. It was warm, her handshake firm and confident.

"Dee Walker."

EJ sat, her long legs touching the seat in front of her. Normally she would have hated being squeezed into a seat like this, but this time she didn't mind at all.

"Did your friends think you were crazy to come on this cruise alone as much as mine did?"

Dee's voice was soft and smooth and sounded like whipped cream. EJ wanted her to repeat the question just to hear her voice again, but asking her to do so would be rude. "How bad was it?" she asked instead, effectively dodging the question.

"They were ragging on me up until the last minute. Like I'd suddenly change my mind and call someone and invite them the night before we set sail." The sparkle in her eyes told EJ that their persistence didn't upset her very much. "What would you have done if I'd called you at the last minute and asked you to go on a three-week cruise to the Caribbean and you had less than twelve hours to pack?"

She answered boldly. "If I'd be sharing a stateroom with you I'd have asked what time you were picking me up." The truth came out of her mouth before she had a chance to censor it.

Luckily the woman chuckled, then replied, "I guess I should get your number in case the opportunity ever comes up again."

"708-555-2863."

This time Dee laughed. "You're quite a risk taker, Ms. Connor. You don't even know if I snore or hog the covers."

The gleam of mischief on Dee's face made EJ's breath catch in her throat. She leaned closer, her lips almost touching Dee's. "What makes you think we'd get any sleep, Ms. Walker?"

Dee turned to look at her, their lips very, very close. Neither of them moved for what felt like forever, and when Dee finally eased her head back, EJ was surprisingly relieved. This time Dee broke into a wide grin.

"You're good, really good," Dee said, drawing out the last two words. Her eyebrows drew together in a frown softened by her next words. "Dangerously good."

The waiter returned and refilled Emery's tea, the clinking of the ice against the glass pulling her attention back from her daydream. The images had flashed through her mind, but each scene was as clear as if it were playing out in front of her here and now.

Dana was looking at her seriously and Emery was about to say something when her chair was bumped from behind.

"Oh my, please excuse me. I haven't had my license for this for very long."

Emery shifted in her chair and turned, expecting to simply accept the woman's apology, but instead came face to face with a woman more than twice her age with a death grip on a dark-brown walker. She smiled as she rose and moved her chair a little more out of the way.

"No problem," she said, eyeing the woman who looked a little unsteady on her feet. "Can I help you?"

"Oh, no, dear, I'm fine. I'm meeting my friend Gladys over there," she said, pointing to another elderly lady at a table not far away. "You two enjoy your lunch," she said, maneuvering her walker through the maze of chairs and tables.

Emery sat down and looked across the table at Dana, who gazed at her as if she were reading her mind.

"Yoo-hoo, Dee. May we join you?" One of the couples who had sat at Dee's table waved at her and approached them. "Yoo-hoo?" EJ looked at Dee and couldn't help but poke fun at the old-fashioned phrase.

Dee leaned close to EJ and murmured, "It doesn't have quite the same effect as when you asked," she said, adding a sly wink to her comment. She motioned to the seats on her left and said to the couple, "Of course, please come and sit down."

"Ladies, this is EJ Connor. EJ, Vivian and Rose Hamilton." Dee pointed in turn to each woman. "They're celebrating their fiftieth anniversary this week."

The women beamed at Dee's mention of their special occasion. Fifty years? Good God. She had rarely been able to stay interested in a woman for more than fifty days. EJ rose out of respect and old-fashioned chivalry and greeted the women. "Congratulations, ladies. You must have been child brides." The women had to be in their early seventies. Vivian, the shorter of the two by at least a foot, looked amazingly like Queen Elizabeth. Rose, tall and regal, reminded EJ of what Grace Kelly might have looked like if she were still alive.

"Vivian always teased me about robbing the cradle," Rose said, complete adoration in her eyes. EJ wondered how something like that happened.

The remaining seats started to fill. "Dee was just telling me how her friends gave her grief about coming on this cruise alone. Something about it being dangerous," EJ added, using the word Dee had used to describe her. Dee elbowed her in the ribs.

"Nonsense, Dee," Vivian said. "You don't need to worry. We've been on cruises like this before and it's perfectly safe."

EJ glanced over at Dee. The expression on her face said she wasn't sure Vivian was right—at least when it came to her.

EJ thought Vivian might pat Dee's hand and say something like, "There, there now." She gave EJ another jab just because the first one felt so good.

"Thank you, ladies, for that note of reassurance," Dee said. "But as a matter of clarity I never said it was dangerous. What I did say was that some women are dangerous." She looked at EJ.

Rose nodded. "I agree, Dee. Take EJ here, for example." All three women looked at her.

EJ played along. "Something tells me I'm not going to like the direction this conversation is headed, but since I'm outnumbered by three beautiful women, I know when to surrender."

"That's exactly what I'm talking about. Not only is she devilishly handsome in her designer suit, but she," Rose pointed an arthritic finger at EJ, "she is charming to boot. And that is a dangerous combination. Very dangerous indeed. You had better be careful, Dee," Rose added in warning.

The lights flickered then dimmed, but not before Dee replied, more to herself than anyone in particular, "Oh, I certainly intend to be."

Chapter Six

The play was better than EJ thought it would be, but her attention kept shifting to Dee. She had been completely aware of Dee the entire evening, and the two or three times their legs touched in the crowded row or their arms shared the armrest, she lost all track of what was happening onstage.

When the lights brightened Dee and Rose started talking excitedly about the play. EJ followed the women out of the theater and through the crowd onto the deck. The cool night air refreshed her slightly overheated body. Sitting next to Dee for two hours and not touching her provided a lesson in self-control.

Dee and Vivian had both stopped to take a breath when Rose jumped in, addressing her comment to EJ. "Vivian can talk all night if you let her, but I don't think you two young women want to spend your first night on board with a couple of old ladies who've been together longer than either of you have been alive." EJ was surprised when Rose winked at her.

Dee turned to look at her, and EJ had no idea what she was thinking. She took a chance and said, "Nonsense," meaning it. "I don't know about Dee, but there's nobody on this ship I'd rather spend the evening with than you three. Why don't we all go up to the main deck and have a nightcap? It's not too cool, and with the stars out like they are, it will be beautiful."

Rose and Vivian looked at each other, and EJ saw Dee nod affirmatively when they turned to her. She extended both elbows to the two older ladies. "Ladies, may I have the honor of escorting you upstairs?" Vivian blushed, Rose giggled, and Dee rewarded her with a dazzling smile.

❖

They weren't alone on the fantail. Several other couples were enjoying the end to their first day on the ship. EJ insisted on getting each of them a drink and balanced them precariously as she weaved around empty deck chairs. She hadn't lied; she was looking forward to spending more time with these women.

"Thank you so much, dear," Vivian said, taking her hot chocolate in both hands. She sipped it carefully before turning to Dee. "Dee, you'd better keep this girl. She's so polite and helpful to have around."

Rose spoke up before anyone could say a word. "You can always use an extra pair of hands now and then." She winked at EJ, who lifted her eyebrows in acknowledgement of the innuendo while Dee recovered from choking on her cocktail.

My, my, Rose, you are a pistol. "Rose, you're a woman after my own heart." EJ tried desperately not to burst out laughing.

"If I were forty years younger it wouldn't be your heart I was after."

EJ teased her. "I'm not sure I could handle you, Rose." To her right, Dee snickered.

"Probably not," Rose replied.

This time EJ had to laugh. Vivian gave her partner a playful slap and Dee shook her head in agreement. EJ couldn't remember having as much fun as she was having right now. Earlier she'd just wanted to spend some quality alone time with Dee but was genuinely surprised how much she enjoyed the other couple's company. She couldn't remember the last time she'd had a conversation that didn't focus on words like *debt to earnings*, *profit*, *amortization*, or *auditor concerns*. She was having a conversation with ordinary people about everyday things. She didn't have to have all the answers or be in complete control. She could just simply relax and enjoy the company of beautiful, charming women.

"I respect the sanctity of marriage so I'll save you from temptation and myself from having Vivian beat the stuffing out of me."

"As you should," Rose said, standing and taking her partner's hand. "Now if you'll excuse us, I'm going to take my best girl and try to remember what lovers do in the moonlight. Come on, Viv. Let's leave these two to discover their own moonlight."

"I'll walk you back to your room." EJ rose from her chair.

"Nonsense," Vivian said, taking Rose's hand. "We're perfectly capable of getting back to our own cabin, and I doubt if anyone will mug us in the hall." Vivian turned to Dee and gave her a quick peck on the cheek. Then she whispered something to Dee that EJ couldn't hear and Dee blushed.

The two women sauntered off and EJ returned to her chair. "Wow," she said to herself as much as to Dee.

"No kidding."

"Those two are full of piss and vinegar, as my Dad would say."

"Your dad and mine must have been brothers, because mine would've said the same thing. I only hope I have half as much spunk as they do when I'm their age. And I hope to be in love with someone as much as they are with each other once in my life."

"Would you like a refill?" EJ asked the question as much to change the subject as to inquire if Dee wanted to continue their evening.

Dee hesitated a second or two, her eyes searching EJ's so pointedly she was starting to feel uncomfortable. Finally Dee answered. "Yes, please."

On her way back with the drinks she saw that Dee had slipped off her shoes and propped her feet up on the chair next to her. EJ was again impressed that Dee was confident enough with herself in her surroundings to make herself comfortable. The women she dated were usually so intent on impressing her or outshining their competition they would never assume the pose Dee had so effortlessly.

"Comfy?" she inquired, setting Dee's cocktail on the table in front of her. Dee had her head back, looking at the stars. The night was clear, not a cloud in the sky to mask the brilliant twinkling of Mother Nature's creations.

"Yes, thank you, my feet were killing me." Dee didn't appear the slightest bit embarrassed. She sipped her drink and several minutes passed before she spoke. "God, it's beautiful out here."

Dee was still looking at the night sky but EJ was looking directly at her when she said, "Yes, you are." Dee turned her head and looked at her. "I never got a chance to tell you that you look stunning in that dress. The color brings out the green in your eyes."

Dee laughed. "Were you and Rose friends in another life?"

"No, why?

"Because she sure has your number. Dangerously handsome and devilishly charming."

She liked Dee's sense of humor. "I believe her words were 'devilishly handsome and charming.' No qualification on the charming," she added. "You said 'dangerously good.'"

"Tomatoes, tomatoes," Dee replied, using the British pronunciation for the latter. Her eyes sparkled. "Let's not quibble over technicalities."

"What would you like to do?"

Dee replied without missing a beat. "Know a little more about you."

She had successfully maneuvered the conversation away from herself all evening. It was amazing how a few well-placed generalities like living in Vegas sufficed for answering a question. At one time EJ thought Rose was going to drill her on exactly where she lived, but the conversation shifted and the moment was lost.

"I could say the same about you," she replied. Dee had been just as adept at keeping any specifics out of the conversation and she was mildly curious.

"I hope you don't think I used Vivian and Rose as a buffer between us."

"Does it matter what I think?" EJ hoped it did.

Dee looked at her as if she were running through a checklist in her mind. "I'm not sure yet."

She wasn't sure what answer she was expecting, but it certainly wasn't that one. "And what are the deciding factors?" They were talking in code and EJ was enjoying the light subterfuge.

"Anyone waiting for you back home?"

EJ answered easily. "Frannie."

"Frannie?" Dee asked cautiously.

"Well, actually her name is Francesca Philippe de la Mound, but I just call her Frannie, or little shit, if she gets into my flowers. She's my springer spaniel."

"Anyone else?"

"Other than my banker, housekeeper, and an assorted array of family members, none of whom live with me, no."

Dee studied her carefully. "You actually expect me to believe that someone so devilishly handsome and charming," she accentuated Rose's words, "doesn't have a girl back home?"

"If I have a girl back home why am I counting the stars with you?"

"Convenience? A surreptitious extended business trip, perhaps?" She looked at Dee seriously. "You've been duped before?"

"No, I haven't," Dee replied seriously. "And I don't intend to be. I don't mess with what belongs to somebody else."

"Well, since I've already sworn my allegiance to the sanctity of marriage to Vivian and Rose, I'll spare repeating myself. Unless you actually want me to say it again?"

The little frown between Dee's eyebrows and the quirking of her mouth were the only indication she was contemplating her response. Her pulse picked up, surprising EJ as she realized she was anxiously waiting for her response. Dee searched her eyes as if judging if she could trust her or not. It felt like an eternity but EJ knew it was only a few seconds before Dee answered.

"No."

"Do you believe me?" EJ leaned forward in her chair.

"Does it matter if I believe you?" she asked, turning the tables on EJ. "I mean, we're here on this boat, soon to be far away from our lives back home. I don't know anything about you and you don't know anything about me. We can share our life stories or we can just enjoy each other."

"And when we return to Ft. Lauderdale?" EJ asked, sipping her drink.

"You go your way and I go mine. More than likely we'll never see each other again. We play by those rules and there's no harm, no foul."

EJ sat back in her chair, relief flooding through her. "So, let me see if I get this straight," she said slowly. "If I understand what you're saying we have a wild and torrid cruise affair, and when it's over, it's over? Did I get that right?"

Dee chuckled. "I don't think I ever said anything about wild and torrid."

EJ's eyes never left Dee's. "You underestimate yourself, Dee. It will be wild and torrid. If you're looking for wine and romance I can do that too," EJ paused, "but remember that we have only twenty more days."

"Other than the first night, you were with me most of the time so I guess you didn't exactly follow doctor's orders, did you?" Dana said sarcastically, pulling Emery's thoughts back to the topic.

She dropped her knife on her plate, the clanging causing several heads to turn in their direction. *Shit, why did she have to go there?* "Ms. Worthington, I know we're in a difficult place here," Emery said in lieu of answering Dana's question. "I mean—"

"I *know* what you mean, EJ...uhh, Emery. And the Ms. Worthington thing. Don't you think we're a bit past the formalities here?"

"Look." Emery put her piece of bread on the side plate and the knife down so she didn't drop it again. "You're a candidate for a job. You're more than qualified, you passed the gauntlet that Jack and his gang of interviewers put in front of you, and here we are sitting across the lunch table together. If I hire you it's because I slept with you. If I don't it's because you slept with me. Either way we're stuck between shit and Shinola, as my dad would say."

"You've already said that. Not in so many words but you did." Dana sat back in her chair, her hands in her lap. "But let's get a few things straight before we go any further. First," she held up her index finger for emphasis, "I had no idea who you were when you approached me on the ship, and by your reaction when you saw me the other day you had no idea who I was either. So that takes care of any ulterior motive. Second," she ticked off the next finger, "you said it yourself—I *am* the best person for this job and you know it. Third, who's going to tell? Fourth, let *me* worry about my reputation, and as for yours, refer to number three. And finally, I wouldn't do anything to jeopardize Martin Engineering or any company, for that matter. I'm not built that way."

Dana's pulse raced as Emery's eyes traveled across her chest before quickly moving back to her face. "And speaking of fucked and screwed," she said, clearly on a roll, "that's what we did. There was very little sleeping together. We were two grown women, unattached and attracted to each other. We had a vacation fling. So what? Big deal. Vacation's over, therefore our fling is over. Isn't that what we agreed to?"

Dee was intrigued with their conversation. They were maneuvering around each other like two fighters sizing each other up, each waiting for the other to make a move. Actually, no one had ever captured her attention as much as EJ had in the last few hours. She was mysterious without being scary, charming without being sappy, witty without being obnoxious, and, most important, she made her laugh. She had to work hard to keep up with EJ's quick brain. But what had really captured Dee's attention was the way her body responded.

When she had first seen EJ looking at her at dinner, she felt as if a bolt of lightning had cracked overhead. A buzz had coursed through her limbs and settled in her groin. A beautiful woman didn't normally arouse her immediately, but something about EJ set her body simmering.

EJ's long, slender fingers were lightly drumming the table. She appeared to be outwardly calm, but the rhythmic movement gave her the impression EJ wasn't as unruffled as she appeared to be.

Was she proposing a wild and torrid cruise affair with this perfect stranger? Correction, perfect, thrilling stranger. Her heart was stuck in her constricted throat. EJ was promising something Dee instinctively knew she could deliver. And she wanted it.

❖

"So, if I understand you correctly," Dee said, turning EJ's last statement around, "I can have either romance or, how did you say it, a wild and torrid cruise affair?" Both sounded fascinating to her. EJ looked at her and Dee saw a twinkle of mischief in her dark eyes.

"I wouldn't say it's one or the other," EJ said calmly. "If you want romance first I can do that, but it shortens the amount of time for the wild-and-torrid part. But if you want wild and torrid," this time when she paused, Dee's heart raced and her nipples tightened, "I'm game."

"Are you always this easy?" Dee asked, trying to lighten the tension in the air around them.

"It depends on the situation."

"Why are you on this cruise? No," Dee said, "why are you on this cruise alone? Someone as devilishly handsome and charming as you could have had dozens of women who would be more than willing to come. No pun intended," Dee added, feeling herself blush at the innuendo. She watched EJ think about her answer to the question.

"I'm here to rest."

Dee practically choked on her drink. "And wild and torrid is your idea of rest? How do I get an appointment with *that* doctor?"

"There are many different kinds of rest," EJ answered smoothly, slipping off her own shoes. She lifted her feet and placed them next to Dee's on the adjacent chair.

"That's a convenient definition. Maybe you should bring me a doctor's release for 'wild and torrid.' I don't want to be responsible for causing you to have a stroke or something," she said, teasing. But the look in EJ's eye told her she had hit a nerve.

"What's on your itinerary for tomorrow when we dock in the Bahamas?" she asked, trying to regain her bearings and erase the seriousness that flickered over EJ's face.

"Nothing."

"Nothing? We can choose from more than a dozen things to do on shore tomorrow and you're doing nothing?" The ship docked in Half Moon Cay at eight in the morning, and passengers could arrange anything from guided tours to water sports to a self-guided shopping expedition simply by stopping by the concierge desk.

EJ repeated, "Nope, nothing. I thought I'd just play it by ear and see what came up."

"Well, I have a full day planned but I do need to eat. How about breakfast on the Lido deck? Say eight thirty?"

"Eight thirty? Up, dressed, and ready for breakfast at eight thirty? I thought this was supposed to be a vacation."

The interest in EJ's eyes told Dee she was teasing so she didn't answer.

"Is that the romance part, a prelude to the wild and torrid, or a polite brush-off? I can be a little dense at times with this sort of thing." EJ was apparently joking.

Dee put on her shoes. "Ms. Connor, I doubt you miss a thing." She stood and didn't answer the question. "Walk me to my room?"

EJ practically jumped out of her chair. "Absolutely."

Emery had to admit that Dana was right. That was *exactly* what they agreed to that first night, and they had followed the script as if they had written it themselves. They'd said their good-byes on deck without either of them looking back.

Dana calmly folded her napkin and placed it on the table to her right. She gathered up her purse. "You need to decide what you're going to do, Emery. I wanted this job before I ever met you, I still want it, and it has nothing to do with the time we spent together. You're either going to hire me because I *am* the best person for the job, or you're not. It's your choice."

Emery watched Dana as she walked away from the table. Why were decisions involving Dana always complicated and painful?

The corridors were nearly empty as they walked down the narrow hall to Dee's cabin on the Promenade deck, three below hers. The difference was more than a little evident. Whereas EJ's halls were carpeted with thick, plush, double-weave carpet, these were flat, industrial-strength, made to withstand thousands of trips by hundreds of people. Offset lighting cast a soft glow in her deck, though these halogen lights burned bright. There were at least twice as many cabins on this deck with very narrow doors. On her deck they could accommodate two people entering while standing side by side. Even the numbers identifying the cabin numbers were vastly different.

When Julia's sister had called and told EJ that the *Seafair* had an unexpected last-minute cancellation in first class, she took it. She didn't need to travel in such luxury, but the suite was the only thing available at such short notice and she had the money to pay for it, so why not? Plus, with the added benefits, a first-class cabin provided that she could rest more. It made perfect sense.

Dee stopped, held on to EJ's arm, and, for the second time that night, took off her shoes. Still grasping EJ's arm, she slipped her hand into the crook and they continued walking. Dee's touch burned right through her suit jacket and sent a flash of heat coursing through her body. Her mouth was dry and she had trouble maintaining the conversation. As a matter of fact she had no idea what they talked about, but whatever it was it kept Dee smiling. EJ hadn't enjoyed the simple act of walking a woman to her door in a very long time.

Rounding the corner they almost ran into a couple engaged in more than a good-night kiss just outside room 4002. The brunette had a tall blonde pinned to the door, her hands fumbling with the doorknob. The blonde had one arm wrapped around the neck of the brunette, and by the way the two were arching and rubbing, EJ surmised the other was in her pants. They needed to get inside the room fast.

Heart pounding at the erotic display, EJ risked a glance at Dee, who looked at her, raised both eyebrows, and said, "Lucky girl."

"Which one?" EJ asked after passing the women. The sound of the door slamming told her they'd somehow made it inside.

"Does it matter?"

She didn't think the question really needed an answer. The image of her and Dee replacing the two women they'd just passed flashed in her brain, and she felt the dormant stirring of desire kick up another notch.

"This is me," Dee stated, stopping in front of the door marked 4015. She withdrew the plastic card key from her small purse and handed it to EJ. Without her shoes Dee was about five inches shorter than her. She took the card but Dee continued to hold it. She raised her eyebrows, questioning Dee's action. The look on Dee's face was more contemplative than teasing.

"What?"

"I'm trying to decide if I should violate my cardinal rule."

"That sounds pretty serious. May I ask what it is?"

Dee answered easily. "I don't sleep with a girl on the first date."

EJ's breath stopped in her throat. Dee had been thinking about having sex with her. "Never?"

"Never." Dee replied firmly. "A girl has to have some standards."

"Very prudent of you. "Do you kiss a girl on the first date?"

Dee answered evasively. "Depends."

"On?"

"On whether I want to."

"And if you don't?"

"I simply thank her for the evening, say good night, and go inside."

"And if you do? Want to kiss her, that is?" EJ asked, still holding on to the card. She leaned closer, anticipating her affirmative decision.

"Then I close the gap between us, reach up, pull her lips to mine, and kiss her."

"Very smooth. No hesitation?" EJ kept her eyes glued to Dee's full, red lips.

"None."

"You're pretty sure of yourself."

"I'm usually right about these kinds of things," Dee said, not sounding the least bit cocky.

"What if she doesn't want to kiss you?"

"*Do* you?" Dee asked instead.

"Yes." EJ replied instantly. She wanted to do much more than kiss her, but that wasn't the question. "We can consider this our first date."

"We can?"

"Yes, because then it's one less time before I can touch you." Emery let her eyes wander lazily over Dee's body.

"I thought you were supposed to be resting on this cruise."

"Well, since you don't sleep with a girl on the first date, I'll be able to rest tonight." She watched Dee search her face, as if trying to make a decision.

Dee stepped closer. "Then I close the gap between us…reach up…and pull her lips to mine." Dee's last word was little more than a whisper against her lips as she did exactly that.

The kiss was light and tentative. Dee's lips were soft, and EJ fought the need to crush her to her. She had been completely enthralled by Dee all evening and wanted more than polite small talk, more than verbally dancing around each other, more than this soft, simple kiss. She wanted to discover every inch of Dee. She wanted to learn where she was ticklish and what made her body sing. Wanted to hear her name come from her lips at the peak of her passion. Wanted to kiss her until it was hard to breathe. Dee's tongue probed her lips and she opened her mouth for more. Dee's tongue was confident and thorough as she explored. EJ gave as much as she got, and when she lifted her head to breathe, Dee stepped out of her reach.

"You are this close," she held her finger and thumb a half inch apart, "to making me say to hell with my rule."

She debated whether to push the issue. If she did, she and Dee would definitely spend the night together. If she didn't she'd go back to her empty cabin more aroused than she'd been in a long, long time. EJ slid the card into the slot and heard the click of the tumblers moving. She turned the knob and swung the door open. The decision was Dee's.

EJ leaned against the doorjamb and crossed her feet at the ankles. She hoped she looked relaxed and casual as she held out the card key. Raising her eyebrows, she said, "It's your call."

Dee took the card key as she passed very close to her and replied, "I hope somebody gets some sleep tonight because I'm sure not going to. See you later." Dee closed the door behind her.

Chapter Seven

Holy crap, Dana, you actually gave her an ultimatum?" Lauren asked over her bowl of egg-drop soup. It was their twice-monthly dinner, which just so happened to be the evening after her lunch with Emery.

"Yes, I did. I was so mad. I'm the best person for this job, and she knows it. She's hung up on this notion about mixing business with pleasure. We didn't mix and I have no intention of mixing it. We had a fling and it's never going to happen again."

"Does she know that?"

"What do you mean?"

"Does Emery know you won't try to rekindle what you two had? She has a lot to lose if you decide to threaten to out her, so to speak."

"And I don't? Do you think I want to have the reputation of sleeping with the boss to get a job? However far that is from the truth. We both know truth is sometimes the furthest thing from reality when it comes to sex and scandal."

Lauren did in fact know. She was an attorney in private practice specializing in children and family cases, and the truth was rarely as clear as it appeared.

"So what are you going to do?" Lauren asked hesitantly.

"I have no fucking clue."

❖

This time when Emery entered the conference room she knew what to expect. The board of Martin Engineering had requested to meet with the final candidate for the open strategy position, and Emery was surprised at how fast Jack and Adam had been able to put this together. She glanced at her Tag Heuer watch. Dana was due in fifteen minutes, but this time she was more than prepared.

Beginning with the chairman, Emery shook hands with each of the eight board members. Including Jack and herself, eight men and two women sat around the large cherrywood table. Sharon Plenner was the lone woman on the board, and from the first day they met, during Emery's interview process, she always had an uncomfortable feeling around Sharon. During the quarterly board meetings, she often caught Sharon staring at her with an expression that looked like she had a bad taste in her mouth. Emery had had several one-on-one meetings and lunches with her to try to build a relationship, but she always walked away with the feeling that Sharon hated the fact that she was a lesbian.

Emery wasn't in the closet by any means, but she also didn't wear a rainbow flag pinned to the lapel of her suit every day. She didn't have a steady girlfriend and, preferring to keep her personal life separate from her professional life, attended social events alone. However, when in turn-around mode, Emery stayed practically immersed in the job, and Martin was no exception. This was the most intense, difficult role she had ever accepted and as such allowed her no personal life. Other than on the cruise, she couldn't remember the last time she had sex, let alone went out on a date.

"Sharon, good to see you again," she said, extending her hand. Sharon always hesitated just a split second longer than was polite, a clear signal that she wasn't thrilled to shake her hand. As if she would catch the I-desire-women germ.

"You look rested," Sharon replied, looking at her critically. When she had informed each board member of her need to take some time off, Sharon had been the most vocal about her doubt that Emery should continue to lead Martin.

"Thank you, Sharon. I am. How is your daughter enjoying Stanford?" Emery quickly changed the subject. Sharon replied and they exchanged a few more brief pleasantries before Marcus Flowers, the chairman of the board, called the meeting to order and Emery stood.

"Thank you all for coming on such short notice. As you know, for the past several months we've been looking for an individual to lead our corporate strategy function. When I first approached the board with my proposal to create this position I said that Martin needed an experienced strategist who can help us identify and deliver on our long-term strategic goals. We engaged Hight & Fraser, a best-in-class search firm specializing in corporate leadership positions, and they found us four excellent candidates. Our own internal selection process slimmed that down to the two candidates I interviewed.

"The individual you will see today is Dana Worthington, our final candidate for the position. Ms. Worthington has a master's degree in organizational management from Columbia University, and an MBA from the Sloan School of Business." Emery recited the remainder of Dana's credentials and work experience up to this point and answered a few clarifying questions.

"As you requested, Ms. Worthington is here to give you a short presentation of her work, her impressions of Martin up to this point, and with that caveat her ideas of where we should focus going forward. We are scheduled for ninety minutes. Any other questions before she joins us?" She looked around the room and, seeing none, nodded to Jack to bring Dana in.

Dana entered the room with complete confidence. Emery greeted her and Dana's handshake was solid and strong. She looked Emery directly in the eyes. Emery's pulse hiccupped and a flash of heat coursed through her. "Good morning, Ms. Worthington. Thank you for coming in."

She introduced Dana around the room, and Dana shook hands with everyone before sitting in the seat next to her. Dana opened her briefcase and pulled out a small notepad and a bright-yellow flash drive.

Dana spent the next twenty minutes giving an overview of several projects she had worked on and had the room's full attention when she talked about her general impressions of Martin Engineering. She was very comfortable in front of these important people, Emery thought. She moved around the room and to and from the screen to emphasize a point. She made eye contact with everyone while she spoke, and every time she looked at her, Emery could swear she stopped breathing until she looked away.

Dana was dressed conservatively yet signs of her personality shone through. Her hair was pulled back in a French braid, the highlights that had reflected the sun a few weeks ago now slightly darker. Her blouse was a pale shade of purple that brought out the matching flecks in the jacket. She was wearing a straight black skirt that fell just above her knees. Diamonds sparkled in her ears and a clunky watch adorned her right wrist. Her fingers were ringless. Dark stockings and black patent-leather pumps made her legs look long and sexy. Emery dug her nails into her palms to keep her attention on what Dana was saying versus the images of those legs wrapped around her.

Dana had this group eating out of the palm of her hand and Emery tried to relax. She was fascinated with the differences between the woman in front of her today and the one she'd known only two weeks ago. They were similar yet nothing alike. Dana was polished, sophisticated, and impeccably put together. Dee was fun, exciting, and simply hot in a pair of ragged shorts and a tank top. Dana was poised, confident, and self-assured. Dee was spontaneous, giggly, and absolutely enchanting.

She could hardly believe this was the same woman. She watched Dana confidently glide around the room. *I know what's under those clothes. I know what's beneath that professional veneer. I know where she's ticklish, what makes her tremble, and how she sounds when she whispers in the dark. I know everything about her and absolutely nothing at all.*

❖

"Gotta minute?"

Emery's back was to her office door and she swung her chair around to see Jack standing hesitantly in her doorway. She had avoided him for the past few days, knowing he was waiting for her answer about hiring Dana. She wasn't any closer to that decision today than she was last week when Dana walked away from the table at lunch. "Sure, come in." She didn't ask her typical "what's up?" because she knew what he would say.

He didn't sit down as he usually did but shifted his weight back and forth on his long legs, a clear indication he was nervous. The other times he struck this pose were when he had bad news, usually in the form of a serious employee incident. Thankfully those were coming far less often.

"Sit down, Jack. You make me nervous when you fidget like that." She indicated one of the chairs on the other side of the desk. Normally when she had visitors she preferred to sit with them on the less-formal furniture in the far corner of her office. She knew what this conversation was about and she wanted, no, needed as much formality as possible. She had to keep this professional and not personal.

"Sorry," he said, almost sheepishly, taking the chair across from her on the left.

She waited for Jack to begin. Normally she was a cut-to-the-chase type of person, but she had been avoiding this decision since the instant she saw Dana in her conference room. God, was it just last week? It seemed like forever and just yesterday at the same time.

"Have you given any more thought to Dana Worthington?" Jack had cornered her the afternoon of her disastrous lunch with Dana and inquired how it went. She was still a little shell-shocked and said something about having to think about it a little more. A little more was now a week later and she needed to make a decision. Dana wouldn't wait much longer.

"Does something about her trouble you, Emery?" Apparently Jack wasn't waiting any longer either. "With every other person you've hired you knew almost the minute you met them if you wanted them. It's not like you to hesitate."

"Has she said something?" Secretly Emery hoped Dana would withdraw her application for the position and take the decision conveniently out of her hands.

"No, nothing other than the requisite follow-up. Do you expect her to?" Jack seemed confused by her indecisiveness.

She glanced at the paperwork on her desk. No, she didn't expect Dana to back down from anything. When they were together she hadn't shied away from anything, no matter how new or physically challenging—one of the activities available in one of the ports, gambling in the ship's casino, or making love in the privacy of her suite.

"Is there something I should know?" Jack asked when Emery still hadn't answered.

Her head shot up at his question and she instantly knew she'd given herself away. Jack was the first person she'd hired when she came to Martin Engineering, bringing him with her from her previous company. They had met on a class project years ago when they were both studying for their MBA at Kellogg in Chicago. They had become instant friends; he was her most honest critic. He knew her well enough to know when to shut up.

The battle whether to confide in Jack waged inside her brain. She wanted to, wanted to have him help her think through this conflict and decision that she couldn't seem to make. What was once crystal clear—do not hire anyone she had a personal relationship with—had become muddied with the introduction of Dana Worthington, aka Dee Walker into her life.

She had never met anyone like Dana and doubted she ever would again. She'd turned her world upside down, sideways, and any number of other geometrically challenging angles. She had, as the tired, yet applicable phrase implied, thrown caution to the wind when she'd met Dana for breakfast the second day on the cruise.

"You know, with one simple move you could have been inside my cabin last night," Dee said after the waitress had taken their order and left.

"I know." EJ was relaxed in her chair, sipping her coffee and crossing her bare legs. She was wearing navy shorts with a crisp white tank top and boat shoes. She had seen Dee look at her legs as she had not-so-casually strolled across the dining room to her table a few minutes ago.

"At the risk of maybe not wanting to know the answer, why didn't you?" EJ admired Dee's honesty and willingness to tackle things head-on. "Because as much as I wanted to, and believe me I wanted to," EJ paused and ran her gaze over Dee's body from head to toe, "I didn't want you to hate me or yourself this morning for breaking your rule."

"Vivian was right, you are quite chivalrous."

EJ felt her face flush with embarrassment. "When did she say that?"

"Last night when you offered to walk them to their room. She whispered it to me when she said good night."

"And that made you blush?" EJ asked easily.

"No, that wasn't it."

"Do tell, Ms. Walker. It must be something good because you're doing it again." The way Dee had reacted made EJ want to know exactly what it was.

"Do you always play by the rules?" Dee asked, trying to change the subject.

EJ tilted her head as if deciding to go along or stay on topic. "When it matters."

"That's an interesting answer."

"Don't you think you're worth it?"

"I have no idea how I should answer that question."

"How do you want to answer it?" EJ asked, and for the second time in less than twenty-four hours Dee's answer really mattered to her.

"Of course I'm worth it," Dee replied honestly.

EJ uncrossed her legs, leaned forward, and looked directly into Dee's eyes. They were sparkling, confident, and direct. "From what I've seen so far, Ms. Walker, I definitely agree."

"Emery? You're starting to scare me." Jack spoke quietly, yet effectively jerked her back to the here and now. She looked at her friend, her human-resources advisor who also happened to bear a striking resemblance to the actor Matt Damon. Shit, she thought. Another battle to add to the constant war she'd been having with herself the last two weeks. If she confided in Jack, told him she and Dana had known each other, he would be obligated to counsel her against hiring her. If she disregarded his advice and hired her, he would be required to report her action to the auditors that hovered in every corner of Martin Engineering these days.

However, if she didn't tell him then he could legally and morally claim, what was it called, plausible deniability? He could honestly say he had no idea. But what would that do to their friendship and the unequivocal trust they shared? She wanted to drop her head into her hands and pretend it was in the sand instead. What a cluster fuck. She had gone on that cruise to rest, heal, get away from the stress of this job, and look where she was now. It didn't get much deeper than this.

"Hire her."

Chapter Eight

Dana didn't see Emery until late in the afternoon of her first day. She'd spent the morning with the requisite new-hire orientation and paperwork, lunch with the other new hires, and the afternoon in the legal and ethics training mandatory for all employees at Martin. Dana had expected all this but was still on edge about her first meeting with her new boss.

She hadn't heard from Emery since her presentation to the board and was surprised when Jack called and offered her the position. It took another two weeks for the drug test and background screening before she was finally an employee of Martin Engineering. It happened exactly one month from the day the ship had returned to Ft. Lauderdale.

It was four thirty and she was settling into her office when she saw movement out of the corner of her eye. She glanced up, expecting to see Adam, the administrative assistant she would be sharing with Emery, but saw Emery herself. Her heart jumped once then settled into a slightly faster-than-normal beat.

"Welcome to Martin," Emery said formally.

"Thank you, it's good to be here." Dana suddenly didn't know what to say next. It would be difficult to act like she and Emery really didn't know each other, but maybe that was true. She knew EJ Connor practically inside and out, but the woman standing in her doorway wearing a tailored royal-blue Chanel suit was a complete mystery.

"Come in." She raised her hand palm up, indicating for Emery to sit in the empty chair across from her.

"Getting settled?" Emery looked around the office she had chosen for Dana. There had been an empty office next to hers and Adam didn't even try to hide his surprise when she told him to move Bob, the head of the legal department, into that one and put Dana three doors down. At the time Emery had thought it was a good idea, but when she saw Dana behind the chrome-and-glass desk she quickly realized that geography wouldn't stop her totally visceral reaction.

She purposely had scheduled back-to-back meetings all day so she wouldn't have a chance to think about Dana being in the building. Her plan had failed miserably as she had to more than once ask someone to repeat what they had just said. This would not be easy. Plus, Dana's desk had a glass front, offering her a complete view of long, tan legs. She knew what those legs felt like wrapped in silk, how they felt as they glided over her skin and captured her. And when she saw Dana cross those beautiful legs a wave of desire pulsed through her. Her jaw slackened, her mouth not far behind.

"Yes, thank you. Adam has been very helpful."

"Did I just hear my name?"

Adam entered the office carrying a large box. He set it on the desk and started pulling out items and handing them to Dana. Emery used the distraction to pull herself together. Holy Christ, this was not going to be hard, it was going to be impossible, she thought as she clenched her thighs. She almost winced at how painfully hard her clitoris was. *Bad move.*

"I've got all of Ms. Worthington's personal information for your flight this week," Adam said, efficiently stacking paper in Dana's printer. "You leave Thursday morning at seven, sorry it's so early." He turned and looked at her. "But you have that meeting with Congresswoman Hecker at four tomorrow, and if you change it one more time it'll look like you're avoiding her. Your return flight is Friday evening at seven thirty, arriving at eleven eighteen. You're booked in adjoining rooms at the Aria and—"

"Adam, take a breath, for crying out loud," Emery finally interjected. "Sometimes you're worse than my mother." She liked to tease him. "Don't you have this written down in one of your colorful folders that we can just look at? Dana just started. She's not used to your rapid-fire efficiency. Sometimes I can barely keep up with you."

And as distracted as she was right now, this was definitely one of those times.

"Sorry." Adam didn't appear to be the slightest bit offended. He picked up the now-empty box. "Of course I do. It's all in the green travel folder on your desk. And this," he turned to Dana and picked up the folder from the corner from her desk, "is *your* green travel folder."

"Everything has a color around here," Emery said, chuckling. "Red is hot, gotta do something with it within twenty-four hours. Blue means do something with it in the next few days. Yellow means to sign, purple is FYI, and orange is read if you have nothing else to do."

"Your orange folder has grown in the past few weeks, and I for one am very happy to see that," Adam said playfully. "It was always empty before you went on vacation."

She defended herself. "That's because I had a company to run."

"And see where it got you? You worked yourself sick." Adam had found her practically collapsed at her desk and got her to the hospital.

"Adam, how many times have I told you not to scold me in front of a new employee, especially on her first day. Please wait at least a week or so. I need to establish some level of respect first."

"Thanks for bringing all this stuff in, Adam. I'm sure I'll need a refresher on the colors, but I think I've got the green one down." She put the folder in her briefcase.

"He's a gem," Dana said after Adam left her office. "Where did you find him?"

"It was more like he found me. He was a temp hired to work in another department, and when my admin at the time kept screwing something up he stepped in and fixed it. He came to me and said I needed someone more efficient and effective, and that he was my man. That was eight years and two companies ago. At times, if it weren't for him shooing me home, I'd probably never leave."

"Well, I'm sure he'll teach me everything I need to know in no time."

Emery glanced around the almost-empty office. Except for the company-provided plant in the corner and three paintings on the adjacent wall, it was pretty bleak. "Whatever you need to spruce this place up is fine. Adam knows all the ins and outs of everything so he'll get you all set up."

Adam returned, this time bearing a huge arrangement of roses, carnations, daisies, and button poms. "Delivery for you, Ms. Worthington. And if I do say so myself, very special delivery." He placed the vase on the corner of Dana's desk.

"Wow," Emery said. "Somebody likes you." And for some completely unjustified reason she didn't like it.

Dana opened the sealed envelope and silently read the card. Emery watched her smile and return the card to its pale-green envelope.

"Just a friend wishing me good luck in the new job," Dana said, since both she and Adam were obviously waiting to hear who they were from, even if it was none of their business.

"Well, when you're through with that friendship, send him my way," Adam said before scurrying out the door.

Adam's comment surprised her. Obviously he hadn't detected that Dana was a lesbian. "Adam is a bit out there," Emery explained when Dana looked surprised. "We're all pretty open around here. We don't flaunt it, or carry billboards, but I refuse to lead an organization that is homophobic. It's simply a nonissue."

Dana regarded her with a thoughtful expression. "Isn't that a bit unusual for a company so entrenched with government contracts?"

"Yes, but it's my company. Actually it's the shareholders' company, but I'm in charge, and I set the standards and lead by example. I don't hide my personal life, but it hasn't come up too many times in conversation either."

"A workaholic?"

"Some would say so." She saw the flash in Dana's eyes that told her she remembered why she had been on the cruise. Thankfully, Dana didn't say anything. "I prefer to think that my job is to turn this company around, and with a company this size and with the hot water it has been in, that in and of itself is more than a full-time job." She wanted to relax but couldn't. The mere fact that she and Dana were in the same room together having a benign conversation unsettled her.

Dana pulled out a pad of paper and uncapped her pen. "So tell me about Columbus."

❖

Columbus tested Emery's will. They sat together in first class, and with the delay on the tarmac the seventy-minute flight ended up lasting closer to three hours. Sitting that close to Dana without touching her was absolute torture. The subtle scent that she would forever attach to Dana floated in the air. They were scheduled to go directly from the airport to their first meeting, and both had dressed for it. Dana had chosen a dark-blue skirt that rode up over her knees when she sat down. Emery wanted to run her hands over the contrasting lighter-blue blouse to verify in fact that it was silk. Of course that urge had nothing to do with the fact that she simply wanted to touch Dana again.

She struggled to maintain focus during the series of meetings as she introduced Dana to the other attendees. The firms that bid on large government contracts were mostly members of the good-old-boy network, with the same names and faces competing for the same contracts. One such firm, Bethel Engineering, was led by James Bethel, a big-mouth boor and general overall sleaze, in Emery's book. He smelled like the stale cigar he constantly held between his thick, sausage fingers and had hair in places she tried not to look at. He leered more than he looked, and she felt the need to shower after every interaction with him. It was the morning break and Jim Bethel was headed their way.

"Emery, who do we have here?" Jim asked, switching his unlit cigar to his left hand as he prepared to shake hands.

"Dana Worthington, James Bethel, president of Bethel Engineering. Jim, Dana is Martin's new VP of corporate strategy." Her stomach churned as Jim turned what he thought were his charms on Dana.

"So pleased to meet you." He grasped Dana's hand in both of his and his fingers moved over the back of her hand. She quickly looked at Dana. Anyone could see that she showed no outward sign of noticing the almost inappropriate gesture. But Emery knew her, and the slight tightening of her muscles around her mouth gave away her dislike of Bethel. *Good girl, Dana. Watch out for this guy.*

"Thank you, Jim. I've read a lot about Bethel. Quite the reputation you have."

Zing!

"All my doing, young lady. I've worked hard to get Bethel where it is today."

"I have no doubt your company is the spitting image of you," Dana said sweetly.

Zing number two.

"Why didn't I know you were on the market, Dana? I can always use someone with your obvious talent under me."

Emery had heard enough and was just about ready to rescue Dana when she spoke up.

"I tell you what, Jim." Dana began to step a little closer to Bethel, almost conspiratorially. "When I'm through with Emery, you'll be the first one I call. Now if you'll excuse me, I need to follow up with Dan Hoskins on something he asked me about earlier."

Zing number three and you are out! She watched Dana stride away and felt a new sense of respect for the woman she'd hired. She was more than capable of handling her own in any situation and had just proved she could slide out of a potentially sticky situation with grace.

CHAPTER NINE

Dana was the center of attention most of the day. A new person rarely entered the mix. Emery watched her quickly grasp the often-technical conversations. She was eloquent yet able to get to the point quickly, asking probing questions that showed she had more than a beginner's grasp of the industry. But when business ended, the inhibitions of the members of this group of men slid away with each round of alcohol.

Here too Dana was not a wallflower, often leading the conversation away from controversial topics, most often personal questions about her. Their table accommodated eight, and sitting across the table from Dana she learned that she was the oldest child, her parents were divorced, her father moved to South Dakota when she was fourteen, and she'd grown up in Denver, where her mother still lived, along with a brother who was an emergency-room physician and a sister who was an actuary. She liked mountain biking, skiing, and running half marathons whenever she had the chance. She was well read, her taste running from John Grisham to Mark Twain. Her choice of music was just as varied, and she loved any movie with a lot of blood in it.

"Emery, how was your vacation?" the man sitting next to her asked. "I heard you went to Fiji or someplace like that."

"Yeah, Emery how did you manage that? You never take time off," the man next to Dana added.

She looked into the cup of coffee she was holding, and in that few seconds she saw the entire three weeks in the smooth, dark liquid. An instant later the images started moving and she realized her hands were shaking. Setting the cup back in the saucer she looked up and directly into Dana's eyes. It was as if she too was remembering everything. Dana's face flushed before she looked away.

"It was the southern Caribbean, not Fiji. They're not even in the same hemisphere, and it was good." She answered vaguely, hoping they would lose interest in her. She wasn't so lucky.

"You went on a cruise, right?"

"Yes." It didn't surprise her how fast news traveled in this tight-knit business community.

"What was the ship? What was the cruise line? What were your ports of call? How long were you out?" The questions kept coming from around the table. She wanted to remember every minute of the cruise, but alone, in the darkness of her room, not sitting around the table with seven other people, one of whom had shared almost every minute with her.

"Come on, guys. You don't want to hear about my summer vacation, do you? This isn't grade school. Let's talk about something else. Pete, didn't you just move to New Jersey?" She was desperate to change the subject.

"Who cares about New Jersey? We want to hear all about *your* vacation, Emery. You're practically an enigma to all of us, and we want to know you're human. Come on, give."

Other than being completely rude, she really didn't have any choice when everybody chimed in with their taunts to kiss and tell. "All right, all right." She avoided looking at Dana.

"We left from Ft. Lauderdale and were out twenty-one days." She intentionally didn't name the ship or the cruise line. She didn't need these guys Googling the lesbian cruise line. She wasn't in the closet but refused to be anyone's titillation. We stopped in the Bahamas, St. Thomas, Martinique, Bonaire, Aruba, and a few other places."

"I hear the rooms on those ships are like cracker boxes," somebody said.

This time she couldn't help but look at Dana. She knew Dana was remembering the first time she saw her cabin. It was at the end of their second evening together.

"Holy shit, this is your *cabin*?"

She closed the door behind Dee and set the key card on the small table by the door. At a little over thirteen hundred square feet, her penthouse verandah suite was larger than her first apartment. It had a king-size bed, oversize whirlpool bath and shower, a separate living room, dining room, dressing room, and private verandah with its own whirlpool tub. She would have been perfectly content with just a shower, a table and chair, and a comfortable bed. However, after meeting Dee she was glad she had a king-size bed.

She was nervous. She'd had women in her hotel room before, and this wasn't any different than some of the nicer hotels she'd stayed in around the world. She'd never used the grandeur of the room to impress them, but for some reason Dee's opinion mattered. She hoped Dee didn't think she was a pompous snob because of the lavish décor.

"Makes my cabin look like a cheap motel room," Dee said, turning in a circle to see the artwork on the walls and the tasteful ornaments on the tables. The windows were floor to ceiling and looked out onto the verandah. "My God, what a fabulous view." She started walking to the verandah, then stopped as if remembering her manners.

"Go ahead," EJ said. "Make yourself at home. Can I get you something to drink?"

"No, thanks, I think I've had enough. May I?" Dee reached for the lock on the sliding doors. When EJ nodded she flipped it and stepped outside.

"This is absolutely beautiful."

EJ followed and watched Dee walk across the verandah and put her hands on the railing. The reflection of the full moon on the calm sea cast enough light to see by, and what she saw took her breath away. Dee was bathed in the soft glow, and she couldn't have imagined a more beautiful sight. It was a scene that the most famous poets and romantics would try a lifetime to describe. Mere words couldn't capture the beauty of this moment.

Even if she could have found the words, she couldn't speak. Dee was breathtakingly beautiful, not just because she was stunning in the blue dress she had chosen for dinner or the way she had swept her hair up and away from her face. The interesting conversation they shared, the challenging way EJ had to think to keep up with her, the way Dee's body moved on the dance floor after dinner completed the perfect package.

When she didn't say anything Dee turned around and studied her for several long moments. Her body crawled with desire. She had been with a lot of women—rich, poor, thin, voluptuous, brilliant, and street-smart—but she had never wanted a woman as much as she wanted Dee. She was intelligent, witty, charming, kind, assertive, and very, very sexy. "You took the words right out of my mouth."

Dee walked toward her, holding her gaze like a magnet, the look in her eyes one of determination and desire. There was no doubt what was going to happen. Dee was going to kiss her. Dee was going to touch her. Dee was going to peel her naked and make her tremble with need.

The kiss was like lightning. Heat shot through her, effectively pinning her feet to the floor. Her head spun and her heart beat so loud she thought it could be heard in the next suite. Dee's lips were like smooth, warm water gliding effortlessly over hers. They were teasing one moment, insistent the next. God, she knew how to kiss, and EJ wanted to kiss her all night.

Her hands were shaking when she touched Dee's cheeks. They were as soft as rose petals, and as she slipped her hands behind Dee's neck and into her thick hair, she deepened the kiss. She had no idea if they stood like that for hours or just minutes, and when Dee broke away they both were gasping for breath. The kiss left her dizzy, wanting more. Much more.

"Is this where you expect me to surrender to your charms?" Dee asked breathlessly, their foreheads touching, their breath mingling into one.

She answered simply. "No." She raised her head and looked directly into Dee's eyes. "This is where I expect you to participate."

This was the moment that could never be repeated. There would never again be the first touch, the first taste of lips on skin, the first sigh of pleasure, the first glimpse of soft, smooth skin, the first slide of fingers through warm, wet folds.

She had had more first times than she could remember, but why was it so different this time? Was it the circumstances, the ship, the anonymity? She didn't know the name of several one-night women, but it had never felt like this. That had been pure mechanics and bodily need. This was something else.

She wanted Dee inside and out. She wanted to ride away in the moment, wanted to go places where they'd never been before, turn sighs into moans, cling to each other until completely spent.

In a few short hours Dee had done something to her that she couldn't explain. She felt a pull toward Dee that she'd never expected. Desire made her knees weak and she trembled in anticipation. She wanted time to stand still and the moment to last forever.

Dee smiled at her then, eyes bright with desire. "Is this when I'm supposed to say yes?"

She could barely think, let alone speak. The blood was racing through her body like it was on fire, most of it settling between her legs. Under her shirt, her nipples were hard, and her body was screaming for release. She gathered whatever strength she had left and took a deep breath.

"This is where you're supposed to say whatever you want to say."

"And if it's no?"

Her heart lurched and a moment of desperation flashed over her. She would die of longing if Dee said no.

"Then I'll somehow pull myself together and walk you back to your cabin. However, you may have to help me because right now I can hardly stand up because I want you so badly." She did her best to smile and was rewarded with a soft kiss, but not before Dee murmured, "Yes."

Dee's kisses shifted from soft and teasing to hard and demanding in an instant. Dee wrapped her arms around her neck and pulled her closer. When their bodies touched EJ responded instinctively, waves of heat coursing through her body, igniting her senses.

She tasted Dee, heard her quiet moans of pleasure, detected every subtle movement of Dee's body. Dee's unique scent filled the air around them and she would forever equate her perfume with this moment. She pulled her lips away from Dee and looked into eyes glassy with desire. Her breathing stopped and the world around her disappeared. Dee was here, in her suite, and she had said yes.

Her hands were steady as she turned Dee so that her back was to her. The breeze coming through the open door blew a few tendrils of Dee's hair across her cheek as she bent and kissed an almost-bare shoulder. She slid her hands up and down Dee's warm, firm arms before returning to the back of her dress.

The only sound in the room was the soft metallic whisper of the zipper sliding down. She covered the exposed bare skin with her lips, and Dee's sighs drowned the sound as the zipper moved down the curve of her back. EJ's hands started to shake as they slipped between the fabric and Dee's tanned skin.

❖

"Shit," Dana said as the cold water splashed over the table. A flashback of all the things they had done together in Emery's suite made her lose her grip on her water glass, and her mind, she thought.

Dee felt the cool air brush against her back as EJ parted the fabric even further, moving her hands around her side and cupped her breasts. The sensation of EJ's hands on her was overwhelming and she couldn't hold back her moan. Suddenly dizzy, she leaned back against EJ's hard body, her head falling back on EJ's shoulder.

"God, you feel good," EJ breathed in her ear. The words made her nipples tight, the huskiness causing shivers to dance across her skin. Desperate for something to steady her, she reached both hands behind her and grabbed the fabric of EJ's trousers.

EJ held her breasts as if they were a set of priceless Fabergé eggs. The tips of two fingers squeezed her nipples, and she arched her back, grinding her ass into EJ's crotch. She was rewarded with a hiss and an equal amount of pressure against her. EJ alternately kissed and licked and nipped at the sensitive skin at the back of her neck. Her legs were getting weaker every moment, and she was afraid they'd soon be in a tangle on the floor.

"I can't stand up much longer if you keep doing that," she said, the strength bleeding from her legs when EJ pinched her left nipple.

"Is that your way of asking me to take you to bed?" EJ replied, repeating her action on her other nipple.

This time Dee's legs gave way and she swayed hard against EJ. Before she was unable to, she straightened and turned to face EJ, whose face was flushed. EJ licked her lips, and Dee slid her fingers under the straps of her dress and let it fall to the floor. She stood there in just her blue lace panties, inches from EJ, the woman who had driven her crazy with desire.

"No, this is how I *tell* you to take me to bed." She took EJ's hand, stepped out of her dress, and led her into the bedroom.

"EJ?" she asked, suddenly nervous. EJ was lying beside her just looking at her as if she were trying to gather her courage. "Is something wrong?" She felt vulnerable and fought the urge to cover herself.

"You are so beautiful," EJ finally said, but still didn't touch her.

She relaxed slightly. "This isn't a look-but-don't-touch situation." Her voice sounded much calmer than she felt. Why wasn't EJ ravishing her like her eyes said she wanted to?

"I'm almost afraid to."

She was shocked. Many lovers had said many things to her in moments like this, but this was definitely a first.

"Why?"

"You're the most beautiful, exciting, sensuous woman I've ever met."

She practically felt EJ's eyes as they roamed up and down her body. "If that's what you think then you'd definitely better touch me." She closed her eyes when EJ finally did.

"EJ, please." Dee whimpered, pulling her face closer and lifting her hips. "Harder," she requested. "Faster," she demanded, and EJ's name echoed in the pale light of the magnificent suite.

❖

Dee slipped out of bed, careful not to wake EJ. It was almost six, and as much as she would have liked another lazy morning in bed with EJ, she had to get back to her cabin, if nothing else for some clean clothes. Not that she'd been in her clothes at all since she'd entered EJ's cabin the night before last. Was it just thirty-six hours ago that she couldn't get out of them fast enough? Where were her clothes anyway? Back then they had fallen at her feet and sailed across the room, and she expected a scavenger hunt to find them.

Quietly closing the bedroom door behind her, she walked into the main room and turned on a small table lamp. The soft light was just enough for her to see her dress laid neatly across the chair next to the couch. She remembered seeing it there yesterday when she and EJ were sitting on the couch having coffee. Her body flushed when she recalled what happened right after that, and she turned to her left to where the large mirror hung on the wall. Her hands started to shake and she quickly pulled on her dress and zipped it up. The flash of memory of when EJ unzipped her dress did nothing to motivate her out the door. She tucked her panties into her purse, then rummaged in the desk and pulled out a piece of paper and pen.

She stared at the blank paper. What should she say? Thanks for the good time? See you later? Let's do this again soon? She settled on a simple "See you later," signed the note, and, with one last look around, left the cabin.

Dana wasn't sure she was still breathing. These guys were grilling Emery, and with every question came a different flashback of their time together. During the cruise they did more than have sex, but no one would know that by reading her mind. She didn't know if the location, the mystery, or the sheer force of their attraction had drawn them together, but everything they did, every tour they took, every adventure in every port either began or ended with them discovering more about their bodies, passions, and desires.

At this moment she couldn't remember much about their ports of call other than how it felt to have Emery caress her before they went ashore or how they hurried back to the ship to once again fall into each other's arms. Sometimes they couldn't wait and Dana had several very quick orgasms in some very interesting locations.

"Oh, man, I've been scuba diving in Bonaire and it is spectacular," the man sitting beside her said. She realized he'd asked her a question and she asked him to repeat it. "Have you ever been…" She must have had a clueless look on her face because he added, "scuba diving."

She froze. Why was he asking her if she had gone scuba diving? Did he know she was on the cruise with Emery? There was no way he could. But then why else was he asking her and not Emery? She forced her face to remain expressionless. She had to remain calm and not look at Emery. She couldn't give anything away.

"Not Dana, stupid." The man to his left slapped the other guy on the arm. "Emery, she's the one that went to Bonaire."

She almost collapsed in relief. Her throat felt like sandpaper and she desperately wanted to drain the glass of water in front of her. She was afraid to, because her hands were shaking so bad she'd probably spill it all over herself. Emery answered the question and diverted the group's attention away from her.

"Yes, it was beautiful. If you'll excuse me, gentlemen," Emery said, pushing her chair back and standing. "I think I'll call it a night."

Dana used the opening to exit the group as well. She was comfortable with the after-dinner chatter about business, sports, or general bullshit with colleagues, but the topic of Emery's vacation combined with the close proximity to her was too unnerving. She was wired too tight and needed to get back to her room and relax.

She hovered by the newspaper stand pretending to be selecting a paper, but in fact she was waiting for Emery to disappear into the elevator. She didn't want to be in the same one with her. It would be too much. Emery was obviously remembering the more intimate aspects of their cruise, and the last thing she needed was to be alone with Emery in a five-by-five-foot, enclosed space. Only when Emery stepped inside and the doors closed behind her did she move into the vestibule and push the Up button.

A few seconds later one of the men joined her, and thankfully he started asking questions about one of Martin Engineering's projects. The faint sound of the bell signifying the arrival of the elevator interrupted her answer. The doors opened and Emery stood directly in front of her. She looked from Emery to the lighted Up button and back to Emery.

"What'd you do, Emery, get on the wrong elevator?" the man asked, clearly amused.

"I guess when I got on, it was going down, not up," she answered sheepishly.

Dana had no choice but to step inside. Emery looked at her with knowing eyes. Just as Dana and the man stepped inside, Jim Bethel squeezed between them. He was practically wheezing in his haste to join them. "What a ride when you think you're going up but end up going down instead. Makes your heart pound, doesn't it?"

He was leering at her, and she refused to acknowledge his poorly phrased innuendo. Jim was standing very close, and she thanked God that Emery had already punched the button for their floor. Otherwise she would have had to reach around him and couldn't have pushed the button without some part of her body touching him.

The ride to the thirty-eighth floor seemed much longer than it had the other three times she'd taken it, maybe it was because Bethel had her pinned in the corner, or maybe because she could see Emery's face clearly reflected in the mirrored elevator doors. She wondered if Emery was remembering another time they were in an elevator, but that time very much alone. It seemed like an eternity before they finally arrived at her floor.

"I'll escort you to your room, Dana," Bethel said. He had barely moved, and if she intended to get off the elevator she would have to brush by him.

"No need for that Jim, I'm on this floor too," Emery said, firmly meeting her eyes. "Her room is right next to mine. We'll see that we both get in safely,"

She looked at Emery, and other than the tightening of the muscles around her eyes, Emery's expression was unreadable. But Emery was clearly pissed and didn't give Bethel a chance to argue.

"Thanks anyway, Jim," she said, somehow sliding around him and exiting without being forced to touch him. "See you all in the morning. Good night." She quickly headed down the hall in the direction of her room. When she heard the ding of the doors closing she risked a glance over her shoulder. Except for Emery walking beside her, the hall was empty.

When they were almost to her door she said, "I can't believe you put up with that shit."

"I beg your pardon?" Emery asked.

"Bethel. I can't believe you put up with his shit," she repeated. "I would have expected you to have ripped his balls off and spoon-fed them to him by now." The thought of Emery doing just that eased a little of the disgust she felt.

Emery stopped in front of her door and said, "He's never been like that. He's a sleaze but he's never stepped over the line. At least not with me. Maybe he knows I'll do just that." One corner of Emery's mouth quirked up in a small smile. It didn't stay long before she frowned. "I'll talk to him tomorrow."

"Oh, no, you don't," she said with emphasis. "I'm a big girl and perfectly capable of taking care of myself."

"I know you can but it's my job—"

"No, it's my job. Actually it's every woman's job to tell creeps like Bethel to shut his mouth, keep his eyes above the neck, and back off." Unfortunately Dana had a lot of experience in doing just that. She was surprised that Bethel was so blatant, but some dogs never learned.

"Dana," Emery said.

"Don't Dana me, Emery. I can take care of myself," she repeated, then realized she was angry, her pulse racing just because she was thinking about Bethel.

"I don't doubt that whatsoever."

Emery's voice was so soft she couldn't help but look into her eyes. They were dark and dangerous and reflected confusion, conflict, and desire. She knew Emery wanted her. She knew that every time Emery looked at her. She was cool on the outside but her eyes gave her away. At least they did to Dana.

A war was raging inside her. The choices were simple: slide into Emery's arms for what she knew would be hours of sexual pleasure or stay completely professional and go to bed alone. No one would ever know. It would be so easy. Their rooms *were* next to each other. Actually they were connecting. If for some reason any of their fellow meeting attendees came knocking at either door with an invitation for breakfast they could step back into their own room. No one would ever know.

"Dana."

Emery's voice was seductive. It was the same voice that made her heart race, her legs grow weak, and it had woken her countless times in the middle of the night. It was the sound of desire, the echo of longing, the craving of a touch, the simple want of another.

In the past few days, she had seen a completely different aspect of Emery, one she never imagined even existed. She commanded a room, was tough, confident, decisive, and always focused. She was the unequivocal chief executive officer of a major corporation. She had the respect of her subordinates and the envy of her peers. She was everything Dana had expected when she agreed to take this job. But the woman standing in front of her now was not that woman.

This woman was EJ, and she ached to be with her again, laugh with her, explore the world with her, and disappear in her arms again. She knew Emery still wanted her, could see it in her eyes and sense it when they were close, even if no one else had a clue. To everyone who knew Emery she was the same composed, driven woman as she was before she went on the cruise. Emery had said it herself. She had a company to think about—hundreds of millions of dollars at stake in contracts, thousands of lives depending on her for their job, their livelihood, their future. Martin Engineering could not be involved in another scandal.

Dana hesitated, their eyes locked. She wanted just one touch. She wanted to feel Emery's warm breath on her neck, smell her scent, taste her mouth. She *needed* just one more. One kiss, one caress, one…Emery's eyes released hers and turned her attention to her lips. Dana swayed toward Emery, toward excitement, toward fulfillment, toward release.

"No!" the voice inside her head shouted. *"No, no!"* echoed her conscience. *"No, no, no"* beat against her chest, commanding her body to stop.

"Good night, Emery. See you in the morning."

Chapter Ten

Emery didn't know if she was disappointed or relieved when Dana stepped into her room and closed the door behind her. She wanted Dana, and with one affirmative gesture the night would look very different from the one she was facing now.

"Good night, Dana," she said to the varnished wood before stepping to her left and entering her own room. She quickly glanced at the connecting door and saw two brushed-nickel deadbolts on the door. The occupants of both rooms had to unlock their deadbolt in order for the connecting door to open. Even from where she stood she could see that the lock that Dana controlled was still firmly in place.

Memories of Dana floated in and out of her brain while she got ready for bed. The shower triggered a memory of another time in the cascading water, and by the time she got out she knew she wouldn't be able to go to sleep anytime soon. She tried to read some reports on Stephenson but couldn't concentrate. She flipped through the channels and found a soccer game between Guatemala and Germany. She kept glancing toward the door, wondering what Dana was doing on the other side.

She glanced at her travel clock and saw that it was only twenty minutes since the last time she'd looked at it. At that time it had read two fifteen. Neither the hot shower nor the sleeping pill she'd taken two hours ago was working. She knew she wouldn't sleep and wondered why she was even trying.

Dana was a few feet away sleeping in that room's king-size bed. Dana had always slept nude but Emery wondered if she did when in a strange hotel. Like Dana, she too slept nude but preferred a pair of large boxer shorts and a white T-shirt when traveling. She had heard too many stories from other travelers of fire alarms, earthquakes, and even a tornado causing guests to run from their rooms in a panic, dressed in only what God gave them.

The image of Dana lying naked in the middle of the bed was causing her sleeplessness. Even though she couldn't actually see her, Emery knew exactly what she looked like.

The faintest light from the reflection of the moon passed silently through the sliding-glass doors of EJ's suite, illuminating Dee's naked body. It was five a.m. and EJ had been watching her sleep for the last half hour. She was lying on her side facing the veranda, her back to EJ. EJ was sitting up against the headboard, one leg bent at the knee, a glass of water in her hand. Dee was beautiful. Her body was curved in all the right places, firm and tight in some and bore the sign of her age in others. Dee didn't try to hide the fact that she was thirty-eight, and that made her sexier than hell. EJ liked a woman who was confident in and out of bed, and Dee definitely met that criterion. She wasn't shy, took control of her own pleasure, and had demanded the same from her.

After only an hour of sleep EJ had wakened, hungry for Dee's touch, her kiss, her demanding caress. Her need surprised her. She would have thought their nonstop lovemaking since entering her cabin shortly after eleven last night would have quenched her desire. By the way her groin throbbed and her fingers itched to touch Dee again, she definitely wanted more.

Giving in to her need she leaned over and kissed the nape of Dee's neck. Dee didn't stir. She kissed the curve of her shoulder, the spot just below her ribs. Again Dee didn't move. She must be exhausted, EJ thought, lightly tracing the path her lips had just traversed. Slowly she explored the curve of her hip, the indentation of the back of her knee, the dimple just above the left cheek of her butt.

EJ shifted on the large bed and moved lower, gently turning Dee onto her back. She glanced up, expecting to see Dee awake, and when she didn't she continued her exploration. Laying soft caresses and barely there kisses on Dee's long legs was like discovering a new landscape. She had covered this ground earlier, but that was in the heat of passion when EJ simply had to touch every inch of her.

This was different. This was slow and deliberate, desire rising like a swift current waiting to gently spill over its banks. She noticed the freckles on Dee's knees, the faint birthmark on her thigh, and the thin red scar that ran almost the length of the inside of her right calf. She kissed it and Dee's legs fell apart, exposing her beauty. She wanted time to stand still.

Dee was absolutely beautiful. Full lips exposed the hard nub of Dee's clit and EJ fought the overwhelming need to taste it. Memories of the feel and taste of Dee overpowered her. Unable to control herself she leaned forward and lightly kissed her. Dee moaned softly but still didn't wake. She explored Dee with long, slow strokes of her tongue. Dee's clit swelled with each pass and EJ's grew hard in unison.

Dee's hips lifted, she moaned again, and EJ felt rather than saw that she was awake. She continued to stroke and slid one finger deep into her warm wetness. Dee gasped and arched her hips even higher.

"Yes," Dee whispered in the fading dark of the night. She reached down and grasped EJ's free hand, their fingers entangling.

Encouraged by Dee's response, she quickened her pace. Dee met her stroke for stroke, beads of her desire filling EJ's mouth.

"More," Dee said urgently.

EJ quickly slid a second finger into her.

This time Dee's response was anything but quiet. "Oh, God, yes." It was part moan, part cry of ecstasy, and EJ fought her own body's need to climax. She focused on Dee, the quick rise and fall of her chest, her arms and legs writhing on the sheets, the vise-like grip of her hand. Faster and faster Dee moved and she struggled to keep up.

Dee's release was an explosion of sensation, affecting every one of EJ's senses. Her name slid from Dee's mouth, the scent and taste of her arousal was sweet, the warmth of her juices filled EJ's palm, and the sight of Dee lying spent on the tangled sheets, chest heaving after her orgasm, drove her to her own release.

"Jesus Christ, Emery," she said out loud, scrambling off the suddenly very empty bed. Her pulse was racing, her hands shook, and her breathing was anything but normal. She paced around the tastefully decorated yet sterile room knowing it was going to be a very long night.

❖

Dana rolled over and looked at the clock. She'd been in bed for an hour but wasn't the slightest bit sleepy. Kicking off the covers she grabbed a bottle of water from the mini-fridge and settled on the couch on the far side of the room. Maybe a change of scenery would do the trick. She closed her eyes and let the cool liquid slide down her throat.

Several hours later Dee had asked, "Are we ever going to get out of this room?" She was sitting on the couch curled up against EJ's side. EJ's arm was a comfortable weight around her.

"Do you have some place you need to be?"

"We're on a twenty-one-day cruise, stopping at twelve beautiful ports of call in the southern Caribbean. I didn't plan to spend a lot of time inside." And she certainly hadn't planned to meet EJ Connor.

"Let me rephrase my question," EJ said, running her hand through Dee's hair. "Do you have some place you need to be that's better than right here?"

"That's a loaded question."

"Then fire away with your answer."

She poked EJ's bare stomach.

"Hey!" EJ exclaimed as she squirmed a little.

She sat up and looked at EJ. They were naked, sitting on a large beach towel EJ had found in the closet. It was after eleven in the morning, and by her count they had made love eight times. But then again, in some instances she wasn't sure when one time ended and another began. EJ's hair was mussed and she remembered the countless times she'd grabbed it to pull EJ closer.

She shook her head and settled back into her spot. They had been sitting this way since brushing their teeth and finishing the pot of coffee that room service had delivered.

"Are you going to feed me today?"

"We just ate," EJ said.

"I don't call raiding the refrigerator and sharing a grapefruit and a container of yogurt eating."

"I suppose you want me to sit up, unwrap my arms from around a beautiful, sexy woman, drag myself across the cabin, take a shower—alone, mind you—get dressed, and escort you somewhere for lunch?"

EJ hadn't moved but made her statement in the same position she'd been in for the past half hour. The vibrations for her voice rumbled in her chest and against Dee's cheek. The amusement in EJ's voice rekindled the flame smoldering inside her. It didn't take much from EJ to fan it into a roaring flame. It was as simple as a touch, a word, a look, or even just a memory.

Dee wasn't a stranger to sex and had always found something exciting about being with someone new. It didn't take much to rekindle new desire, but this was the first time she absolutely could not get enough of someone, and that someone was chuckling in her ear.

"Who said anything about showering alone?" She felt the immediate hitch in EJ's breathing and the increase in her heartbeat.

"Why didn't you say that in the first place?"

EJ stood up, grabbed her hand, and pulled her into her arms. Her kiss was passionate, and their warm bodies pressed against each other fueled Dee's desire. Dee deepened the kiss and sucked on EJ's tongue, pulling it into her mouth. She bit lightly, then began sucking and nipping EJ's neck. Her hands were equally busy running over the soft contours of EJ's hard body. She grabbed EJ's ass and straddled her thigh, pulling them closer. EJ's hands were on their own quest for pleasure and tweaked her nipple just hard enough for her to moan.

Dee wasn't sure if she was moving or floating, but when EJ pressed her back against the wall she didn't care. EJ's hands were everywhere, and Dee raised herself up to ride her lover's solid thigh. She struggled for breath. "I thought we were taking a shower."

"Later," EJ mumbled against her mouth breathlessly. "I need you right now. The shower will come right after you do."

She gasped when EJ slid her fingers between them. Now, instead of riding EJ's leg she was on her fingers. And what magical fingers she had. She dropped her head onto EJ's shoulder in complete surrender and caught their reflection in the mirror at the end of the hall. They were intertwined as only two women could be. EJ's tall body had her pinned against the wall. Her arms were wrapped around EJ's neck, her leg pinning EJ's for support and stimulation. Lines and curves intersected, limbs overlapped, and they thrust against each other. The sight was raw, primitive, and sensuous. One second later Dee exploded, her orgasm ripping from her throat, the sound smothered in EJ's.

"Holy shit, what was that?" she asked between gasps of air, trying to refill her depleted lungs. Her head rested in the crook of EJ's neck and thankfully EJ was still supporting her.

"Awesome," EJ answered, her own chest heaving for air after her own climax.

Dee trembled from an aftershock of her powerful orgasm. "Hold me." Her voice was barely above a whisper.

"I've got you," EJ said, tightening her arm around Dee's waist. Her hand was still between them and she inhaled sharply when EJ's fingers started to move again.

"You are so fucking sexy."

Dee felt the surge of yet another orgasm approach, and she lifted her head to again see their bodies coupled in the mirror. This time, she didn't try to suppress her scream.

Chapter Eleven

Dana ordered another refill of coffee from the waitress that hovered closer to her table than necessary. The waitress had held her gaze just a little too long after she placed her order, and even through her grogginess, she detected interest. She hadn't slept much the night before. Knowing Emery was on the other side of the door was not what she needed to facilitate a good night's sleep.

Her eyes felt like sandpaper, and it had taken several attempts before she could get her contacts in. The cold shower helped a little, and she hoped that her breakfast of bacon, eggs, and oatmeal would give her the energy she desperately needed.

"How is a pretty little thing like you gonna eat all that?"

Dana groaned inwardly, recognizing the voice of James Bethel. He was the last thing she needed this morning—or any other time of the day. She put on her best meeting smile and looked up.

"Good morning, Jim." She didn't answer his question or say anything to give him any reason to join her. He didn't get the hint.

"Mind if I join you?" He didn't wait for her to reply as he pulled out the chair across from her and sat down. His leg immediately made contact with hers and she knew it was not accidental.

Her appetite slipped away like the steam rising from her coffee cup. She would have welcomed any attendee of the conference to sit at her table except Jim Bethel. If her tired body didn't need the fuel and she didn't want to give him the satisfaction of affirming his stupid comment, she'd make up some excuse and leave. As it was she simply said nothing.

"Coffee, and I'll have what my beautiful breakfast companion is having," Bethel said as he waved his arm at the waitress. Since Bethel was not looking at her, the waitress frowned at Dana.

"Jim," Dana said, trying to sound casual. "I appreciate that you're making me feel welcome here at the conference, and I certainly don't mean to sound ungrateful, but I would prefer you stop with the inappropriate comments, looks, and touches." If she didn't call him on his behavior right now, it would be harder if not impossible to stop later. Unfortunately she had been down this road too many times, and it still pissed her off when it happened. She wouldn't dream of saying something like that to a man or even another lesbian in a business setting.

"What are you talkin' about, doll? I don't mean no harm. I just call 'em as I see 'em." Bethel had slipped into what he probably thought was his good-old-boy accent. "You have to admit that you like it when a man acknowledges how pretty you are."

She put her fork down and looked at the nametag of the waitress filling Bethel's cup. "Pam, would you please stay for a minute?" When the waitress nodded, Dana said, "I'm Dana Worthington and this is James Bethel." Then she looked Bethel squarely in the eye. "I'm going to tell you this one more time, Mr. Bethel. I do not appreciate or want to hear any more references to my body, what I eat, how much I eat, what I'm wearing, or anything remotely personal about me. I do not appreciate or want to see your eyes anywhere on my body except my eyes or looking at me in any way other than professionally. Do not touch me again, and take your leg away from mine right now. I find your remarks, leers, and innuendos unprofessional, in poor taste, and extremely offensive. Do I make myself clear?"

She maintained eye contact with Bethel. If she wavered at all he would take it as a sign of weakness and her statement would lose its impact. She watched his eyes spark in anger, then just as quickly tame. She calmly waited for his reaction.

"I didn't mean any harm, Dana," he said. His apology was lukewarm and lacked sincerity. "I'm sorry if you took it wrong."

"*I* didn't take anything wrong, Mr. Bethel. Now I don't want this to impede our professional relationship or the working relationship of Bethel and Martin Engineering, but I will not tolerate any other inappropriate looks, words, or touches. Do I make myself clear?" She repeated herself for emphasis.

He put his napkin on the table and stood. The waitress had to step back or risk being knocked over by his bulk. "I seem to have lost my appetite," he said just before he walked away.

Dana breathed a sigh of relief but knew it would be short lived. Bethel had neither apologized for his actions nor acknowledged her cease-and-desist demand. This would not be the last she heard from Jim Bethel.

"Wow, you cut him off at the knees," the waitress said admiringly.

"Men like him probably think it's his balls," she said sarcastically.

Pam snickered, and when Dana asked for her phone number she gave her a I'm-definitely-interested-in-you smile. Dana quickly set her straight. "In case I need you to verify this conversation." Pam walked away obviously disappointed.

"What was all that about?" Emery asked from behind her. She at least was polite enough not to sit down unless invited.

"Just clearing the air with Bethel. Nothing for you to worry about."

"It didn't look like that from where I was standing."

Dana glanced at the front door of the restaurant, ensuring that Bethel had left before she indicated for Emery to take the seat in front of her. She waited for Emery to settle in. "Nothing for you to worry about." Emery started to reply but Dana stopped her. "At this time. If I need your political muscle I'll let you know. Have you had breakfast?" She caught Pam's eye and signaled her to return to the table.

"I had something in my room," Emery replied.

"Coffee, then?" she asked. As hard as Dana knew it would be, she enjoyed Emery's company.

Emery's eyes flashed and she knew her innocent question had sparked a memory. It was probably the same one she had.

"I can't do anything without at least two cups of coffee."

Dee chuckled. "You sure could have fooled me." They were on top of the tangled sheets, Dee snuggled against EJ. The ceiling fan spinning slowly above their heads cooled their hot, sweaty bodies.

"You know what I mean," EJ said, slapping her playfully on the butt, then returned to gently stroking up and down her arm.

The beat of EJ's heart was strong under her palm. After several minutes it was finally settling down into a normal cadence. Her own was still beating a little faster than normal, a tribute to just how powerful her orgasm had been. She poked EJ in the ribs. "I just asked if you wanted to soak in the Jacuzzi tub, not swim the English Channel."

"I repeat myself. Without my coffee I might drown."

She rolled on top of EJ, sitting up and straddling her. They were both naked, their skin-to-skin contact sending a jolt of desire crashing through her yet again. "Does that mean I'd get the chance to be your knight in shining armor and rescue you?" she asked playfully.

EJ lazily took her time moving her eyes over Dee's bare chest and below. When she finally looked her in the eye, Dee's desire kicked up a notch. The look in EJ's eyes was one she had seen many times in the last few days. It held passion, promise, and fulfillment.

"You're definitely not a knight and you're hardly dressed for it." EJ's voice was husky, the same tone she'd heard many times during the night. EJ's wandering hands were getting pretty close to where Dee wanted them to be.

Slowly she leaned over EJ. Her nipples skimmed EJ's chest, sending shock waves through Dee yet again. Her juices allowed her to slide over EJ's pubic bone with little difficulty, and Dee couldn't hold back her moan. "Well then," she murmured, just before placing several light, teasing kisses on EJ's ready mouth. "Far be it from me to keep you from getting what you need." She kissed EJ again, this time a little more seriously. EJ reached for her but she reached for the phone on the bedside table instead. She punched a button.

"Room service? This is EJ Connor in the Penthouse suite. I'd like a pot of coffee, please, two cups. How long? Fifteen minutes? Perfect." She hung up the phone. "Now, where were we?"

"I don't want to intrude on your breakfast," Emery said hesitantly. "I saw you with Bethel and—"

"And you thought I needed help." She was pissed off and didn't bother to hide it. Emery had the grace to blush a little at being so obvious. "I told you before, Emery. I appreciate your help, but I'm a big girl and I can handle the likes of Bethel. And no, you are not intruding on my breakfast. As a matter of fact, this is cold and I'm going to reorder." She motioned Pam to the table and ordered again. "Coffee?" She repeated her question, looking at Emery.

Pam brought Emery a fresh cup and refilled hers. "So what did you think of the meeting yesterday?" she asked, steering the conversation to a safer topic.

"This was very different." Emery added cream and one sugar to her coffee.

The action was very familiar, and Dana told herself to stop looking at Emery's hands and thinking about all the other times they'd shared morning coffee. "How so?" she asked, trying to get her head back on the topic she'd brought up.

"This builder normally doesn't work like this. Usually the company sends out the RFP and we reply with our quote for each line item. Gremlin Aerospace has a new CEO, and I guess he's trying out something different instead of the standard request-for-proposal format."

"It is a bit unusual, but hey, I guess if it works for them that's all that matters."

While Dana ate her breakfast they talked about the strategy Martin might take to secure this bid. Emery was again impressed with Dana's intelligence. She captured concepts quickly, suggested innovative solutions, and didn't hesitate to ask questions if something wasn't clear. She easily displayed her thoughts. She frowned when she was concentrating as effortlessly as she smiled. She had a habit of pursing her lips when she was thinking, and even now she was making notes on a spare napkin.

Dana was impeccably dressed this morning in navy pants with a royal-blue sweater. The matching suit jacket was draped carefully over the chair next to Emery, and a quick glance showed the label of an exclusive boutique in New York. Emery recognized her shoes as Cole Haan for women, and the wide band of diamonds on the ring finger of her right hand was large enough to be tasteful and subtle enough to say successful. Her nails were painted a calm shade of peach, accenting her long fingers. The fashion-conscious would consider her watch a fashion faux pas, but it fit her character perfectly.

A Breitling Navitimer, it was definitely not from the smaller woman's line. It looked heavy and sturdy on her wrist. On any other woman it would have looked ridiculous, but on Dana it simply looked sexy.

"I'm sorry, what did you say?" she asked when it was apparent Dana was waiting for an answer.

Dana looked at her questioningly. "I asked if you were ready to go. The next session starts in fifteen minutes."

"Uh, yes, sorry," she said quickly, berating herself for losing focus.

In the hotel lobby they elected to take the stairs adjacent to the large aquarium instead of the escalator to the third-floor meeting rooms. Yesterday when Emery had checked in she noticed that the aquarium contained fish similar to those they had seen while scuba diving in Bonaire.

Don't go there, she told herself, carefully putting one foot in front of the other on the next step. Dana was beside her and one step above, and Emery almost tripped when she let her eyes drift to her backside. Dana didn't need Spanx, uplifting undies, or any other artificial ass-contouring equipment. Emery knew what was under the linen pants and it was perfect.

During the break she noticed that Dana avoided being anywhere near Jim Bethel. Her evasion wasn't blatant enough to be apparent to anyone who didn't know the situation, and Emery admired the way she handled herself. She watched as Dana spoke to several groups of people and handed out her business cards to others.

But the green monster of jealousy gripped Emery's stomach every time one of the men looked at Dana in *that* way. What was it about the opposite sex that made them believe they had permission to ogle every woman they found attractive? Emery had once read an article about how some scientists believed this tendency had become ingrained in a man's DNA over centuries of adaptation. The theory was that for man to continue to exist and not become extinct, males were constantly on the prowl to mate. She'd laughed when she read the research report and viewed it a convenient excuse for men who wanted to stray. Her own sex wasn't immune to cheating, but to say it was genetic was pure bullshit.

Finally the day was over and she and Dana were in a cab headed back to the airport. She had a throbbing headache, and the flight back to San Diego was not going to help. Neither was sitting next to Dana again. The flight over had been stressful enough, but now after spending two days with Dana the return trip would be unbearable.

She gazed out the window on her side of the cab. She was being rude, but she could only answer Dana's questions or comments with monosyllabic responses. After watching Dana all day yesterday, her sleepless night, and another six hours of being asked, "Where is Dana," she was exhausted.

"Emery," Dana said from her left.

"What?" She knew she sounded pissed off, and frankly she was. In addition to the constant awareness of Dana and fighting the memories of the cruise, she was angry at herself for not being able to keep the two separate. Dana as Dee kept infiltrating her mind and she had no idea how to stop it. But she had to. Her career and that of Dana's and Martin Engineering depended on her ability to focus and lead the company forward.

In her entire professional life she had never been as distracted as she had been since returning from the cruise. She was confident and secure in her single-minded drive regarding what she needed to do and had never before been tempted to deviate from that path. Work was work, and she devoted one hundred percent of her attention and energy to it. Even when she played, which wasn't very often, she was thinking about work. And look where that had gotten her. Half dead with doctors' orders to rest, and instead she ended up meeting the fascinating woman next to her.

"Have I said something to upset you?"

She couldn't resist Dana's soft tone, which added to her self-imposed anger. She wanted to blame Dana for her growing lack of self-control but it wasn't her fault. "No, of course not. It's just been a long couple of days. I'm a little tired and have a lot on my mind."

Emery watched as Dana decided whether to push the issue or let it go. She was grateful when the cab driver announced their arrival at the airport and she could busy herself with getting through the throngs of other Friday-night travelers.

They didn't say anything to each other as they maneuvered through the security checkpoint and the myriad shops and restaurants that dominated every airport in the world. Dana excused herself to stop in to a bookstore, and Emery walked down the long corridor to their gate.

The flight was as quiet as the cab ride, Dana with her nose in a book and Emery pretending to read. After gathering their bags and disembarking she made polite small talk as they headed for the parking lot.

"Are you in the garage?" she asked, pointing to the massive structure in front of them.

"No, someone's picking me up," Dana replied, looking to her left, then her right at the line of cars waiting at the arrival curb. "There she is." Dana waved and picked up her briefcase. "See you Monday."

Dana hurried down the sidewalk and right into the arms of a stunning woman standing beside a red BMW. The woman was tall, blond, gorgeous, and pregnant. They hugged tightly for several seconds, and the woman gave Dana a quick kiss on the lips before dropping her bag in the trunk.

CHAPTER TWELVE

Emery's heart stopped. It wasn't a jaw-dropping passionate kiss, but it was more than a casual-friendship kiss. Did Dana lie to her on the cruise about being single? Emery knew next to nothing about pregnancy, but even with her limited knowledge she realized this woman was far too pregnant to go on the cruise. Had they already paid for the tickets and then discovered she was pregnant? That made no sense. Lesbians don't *discover* they're pregnant. It takes planning and timing, all of which meant they would know *exactly* when something like this would happen.

Maybe it was the woman's gift to Dana—one last vacation fling before she got tied down with a baby. Maybe the woman had just thought Dana was on an extended business trip. That could happen. She knew a man who had a complete other family in another country. He spent two weeks a month in Tokyo and two weeks in the States. He had somehow managed to keep his two lives separate for eight years until his car slid off an icy mountain road in Colorado. Then the shit hit the fan when both wives claimed his death benefits.

Dana would never do something like that, she thought as she watched the car drive away, its red taillights getting smaller and smaller until they were barely a speck in the night. Would she? Emery thought she was a good judge of people and character, but what did she really know about Dana? She'd known nothing when they met and next to nothing about her personal life when they said good-bye three weeks later.

Her normally clear, focused brain was so muddy she couldn't remember where she'd parked her car. After fifteen minutes of wandering around two different levels of the garage she remembered she had written her space number on her parking ticket. It was habit for her to do this because she traveled so much she often forgot where she'd parked without it. Eight minutes later she paid the clerk at the exit booth and was on her way home still thinking about Dana, the woman, and the kiss.

❖

"How was your trip?" Lauren asked.

Dana had put her car in the shop for some much-needed service work while she was in Columbus. "Pretty good, really interesting. But I'm not going to bore you with the details."

"You're right. I probably wouldn't know what you were talking about anyway."

"Don't sell yourself short, Lauren. You're one of the smartest women I know."

"It's not that. Lately I can't seem to keep track of anything anymore." Lauren maneuvered the sleek car through traffic.

"You're six-and-a-half months pregnant with your first baby. Duh. You're not supposed to keep track of anything other than getting ready for her to be born."

Lauren chuckled and dropped her hand to her stomach. She barely fit behind the steering wheel.

"Tell me about it. I'm way done with being an incubator. There's no more room in this inn and this baby needs to vacate the premises." She pointed at her stomach.

"What did your doctor say at your last checkup?"

"She said a lot of first babies are late, but that doesn't mean ours will be."

"Are you ready for this?"

"Yep. The crib is up, diapers are stocked, baby clothes washed and folded—"

"That's not what I'm talking about," Dana said quietly. "Are you *really* ready for this?" Dana didn't know if she'd ever be.

Lauren risked a glance at her and laughed. "Well, if I'm not, it's way too late to go back now."

"Yeah, I guess you're right." She laughed. "It was kind of a stupid question, wasn't it?"

"Kind of, but I forgive you. How about you? You're still going to be in the delivery room, aren't you?"

"Of course I am. Somebody has to catch Elliott when she faints." Lauren's spouse had a dreadful fear of blood. Every time they talked about the labor and delivery, Elliott's face paled and she looked like she would pass out.

"Are you ready to be an aunt?"

Dana corrected her. "An honorary aunt."

"Details, details," Lauren said, waving her hand as if they were trivial.

"You of all people actually said that? You're a lawyer, for God's sake. Details are your life."

"Yeah, and my life is about to change drastically. I'm to the point that I can only focus on the big things and hope it doesn't get much bigger than this." She rubbed her baby belly.

"How's Elliott doing?"

"Exactly as you'd expect. Hides in her work when it gets too overwhelming. But she's there when I need her."

"Uh-huh," Dana said doubtfully.

"No, really, she is. She's come to every doctor appointment with me, every ultrasound, every blood test, everything."

"But…"

"But she's scared shitless."

"You've taken care of babies before. How many foster children have you two taken in over the years? A bunch have been babies."

"I made the same argument and she isn't buying it. She says this is different because this is *our* baby, not one we're just looking after for a while. She's so afraid she's going to drop it or do something to break it." Lauren turned onto the ramp to the freeway.

"You know she really loves you," Dana said wistfully.

"That's what she keeps telling me. Maybe one of these days I'll really believe it."

"What? You don't believe—"

"No, no, of course not. I know she loves me. I feel it. At times I'm sitting across the breakfast table and think this woman really loves me. She loves *me*. And I love her. I can't even imagine my life without her. I can't even remember my life before I met her.

"I was lying in bed the other night not able to sleep, of course, and I realized I'm actually having a baby. *I'm* having a baby, Dana. Can you believe it? Elliott and I are having a baby. I'm committed to her for the rest of my life. I mean if something happens to us—"

"Lauren, don't talk like that. You two love each other."

"I know. I'm pregnant and emotional and have a right to say stupid things. But a baby changes things. It makes everything different. I will be connected to Elliott for the rest of my life. Because of this baby."

"And…" Dana asked carefully.

"And I am so happy. I can't even describe it."

Dana let out a silent sigh of relief. Lauren and Elliott had the most solid relationship of anyone she knew. She had never seen two people so much in love. She'd watched them at a party one night. Each one was talking to her own separate group of people yet each knew exactly where the other one was. Their eyes were constantly moving until they found each other.

She wanted that connection at least one time in her life. Was it too much to ask? She wanted someone to love her like her two dear friends loved each other. When she was younger she dreamed about it, knew it would happen. It was just a matter of time till she met the right woman. But now, almost twenty years later, she was beginning to wonder if she would find a woman that still took her breath away eight years later as much as the first time they met, the first time they made love, and the ten-thousandth time they made love. She knew it wasn't too much to ask, but asking and reality were sometimes two very different things. But she was determined not to settle for anything less. The image of Emery flashed in her mind.

"So how was Emery?" Lauren asked, merging smoothly onto the freeway.

"Fine, very helpful, introduced me to all the right people, set the stage, paved the way a little bit." Dana answered evasively.

"That wasn't what I was asking and you know it."

"Lauren."

"Come on, Dana. I mean, my God, you two were together for three weeks. You had sex what…dozens of times, hundreds of times?

"Lauren!" Dana replied loudly. "Hundreds of times?"

"Dana, I've seen Emery, so I have no doubt…uh-huh…hundreds of times." Lauren shook her head in confirmation.

"You know, Lauren, we did things other than have sex." But sometimes she had a hard time remembering exactly what.

"Oh, yeah, I'm sure you did. Let's see, got ready for sex, thought about sex, woofed down your food so you could go back to your cabin to have sex, took a shower and had sex, took a bath and had sex, went snorkeling and had sex."

"Lauren," Dana said when she stopped to take a breath. As much as she wanted to protest, she knew Lauren pretty much had it spot-on.

"Elliott and I went on one of those cruises." Lauren continued as if Dana hadn't said anything. "And I know what we did and we'd been together years. I can just imagine what it was like just meeting each other."

"Jesus, Lauren, you make it sound like it was nothing short of a sexapalooza." Images of some of the many times, ways, and places she and Emery did have sex flashed in her head like a strobe.

"Dana, you are talking to a woman who is very pregnant. I swear the instant I got pregnant I became so horny I practically jumped Elliott every time she came into the room. Not that she minded." Lauren blushed.

"You know, Lauren, you're my BFF and we share just about everything, but that's way too much information. Now I understand that you're pregnant, your hormones are crazy, and your emotions are all over the place, but I don't really need to know that about you and Elliott."

"Yeah, well, after this little bundle arrives I'll never have sex again."

A wave of heat flashed over her, and as much as she wanted to open the window or fan herself, she would never live it down from Lauren. "Can we just change the subject and talk about something else?"

"Then let's go back to my original question."

"Any my original answer was she was fine."

"She didn't—"

"No, she didn't."

"And you didn't—"

"No, I didn't."

"But—"

"No, Lauren, no *but*s. I don't know how many times I have to tell you." And one of these times I'll convince myself, she thought. "Emery and I have a strictly professional relationship now. Neither of us wants anything else and there can't be anything else. We have too much to lose. I have a job to do and Emery hired me to do it. And it doesn't include sleeping with the boss."

"Well, it wouldn't exactly be sleeping with the boss."

"That is exactly what it would be. Emery is my boss. She's not my girlfriend, she's not my lover, she's not anything other than my boss. And she's going to be nothing other than my boss."

"You know I don't understand."

"I know you don't, and I can appreciate that, but please drop it," she said firmly.

She was having a difficult time convincing her body that was exactly what it needed to do. Absolutely nothing other than her job. Her body and her visceral memories, however, weren't listening. If she wasn't looking for Emery practically every minute since she'd gotten off the damn ship, she was thinking about her. And during this first week of employment, if she had a dollar for every time she thought of her boss and every time she remembered any of their time together on the cruise, she could retire today and not worry about money for the rest of her life. *What in the hell was I thinking when I accepted this job?*

❖

As the weeks went by, Dana felt more comfortable with her role in Martin Engineering. She had traveled to several of the sites around the country, spoken to dozens of people, asked thousands of questions, and taken reams of notes. She was beginning to think she finally had a grasp on what was going on—the challenges, the market conditions—and ideas of what she needed to do were starting to become clear in the back of her head.

She woke every morning excited about going to work, knowing she could make a difference in the success of this company. She loved working for Emery. She loved watching her work, the way she thought about things. The way she cut to the chase, weeded through all the crap and the bullshit and made decisions. She gathered input from her team, they discussed things, at times quite contentiously, but at the end everyone had reached consensus and agreement about the direction they were moving.

She hadn't seen much of Emery, her own visits around the world taking most of her time. But when Dana was alone in her hotel room in some strange city, just before she closed her eyes she thought of her. She remembered her. It was as if she could taste her again. Feel her touch again. Feel the heat rise in her again.

Dana had taken pictures of the cruise, and once the whole Emery/ Martin situation became clear she'd loaded them in a password-protected folder on a flash drive. During these times in these obscure hotels in these no-name towns she loaded them on her personal iPad and scrolled through the memories.

Other than the one a street vendor had taken of them, there were few pictures of Emery. She somehow knew that Emery wasn't comfortable preserving their time together. Now it was pretty obvious why. But the pictures she did have were of the places they went, the things they did. Pictures of parasailing, Emery beside her in the tandem seat. Underwater pictures in Bonaire and the Bahamas as they scuba-dived together. And then there was the view from the top of the cliff where they had hiked to have a picnic. The picnic that lasted only ten minutes before they were in each other's arms yet again.

She formatted these pictures to run as a slide show. She certainly hadn't intended it be, but her cruise and the time she'd spent with Emery were a very big part of her life. She couldn't very well file them away in a drawer. She supposed she could, but she didn't want to and wasn't going to. As she watched these pictures transition in front of her she ached for Emery's touch, their soft whispers in the dark, the bold looks in the light of day. During this time she imagined Emery's hands were on her, caressing her, squeezing her nipples. Emery's long skillful fingers moving inside her, thrusting back and forth until she came in a powerful orgasm screaming Emery's name in the empty room.

Chapter Thirteen

I'll be right there." Dana hung up the phone, grabbed her purse, closed her computer, and was across her office and at her door in ten quick steps.

"Adam, clear my calendar for the rest of the day. Something's come up and I've gotta go."

"Is everything all right, Dana?"

"Yes, and I hope it stays that way. It's personal, I have to leave."

"Will you be in tomorrow?"

"I should, yes." Dana punched the button on the elevator panel. "I'll call you later," she said to the doors closing in front of her.

The drive across town to Women's Hospital took forever. Lauren was in labor, and even though Elliott told her it would be hours before she delivered, her best friend was having a baby and she was going to be there.

Elliott had been right, and seventeen hours later Dana was holding the little girl who looked exactly like her mother. Dana had always known she wanted children. It didn't matter if they were natural or adopted, and she knew it sounded corny, but someday she wanted to hear the pitter-patter of little feet running around her house.

But did she want to be a single mom? Of course not. She wanted to share the experience with someone, and not just anyone. The co-mother of her children would have to be completely committed and have the same values and ideas about childrearing that she did. Yes, they would compromise but the overall foundation would have to be solid.

Holding baby Grace, she had an overwhelming feeling of protectiveness for this child. If anything happened to Lauren and Elliott, Grace would be hers. They had talked about it and the paperwork was signed. Yes, Grace wasn't hers, but every child deserved to have the safest life possible and the love of the people around them. Dana thought about the hours she spent on her job. Not just the hours in the office, but the hours in airplanes, after-hours dinners, and the countless ones she spent at home reading, catching up, or preparing for the next day. She loved her work and didn't mind the time and commitment it took to be successful. But if she had a child, no, *when* she had a child that would change. Her children would become her top priority.

What would Emery think? She was completely dedicated to her job and didn't accept anything other than that attitude from her staff. The men had wives, and the women either had grown children or were childless. If she was still at Martin Engineering...would she still be there?

The thought of leaving Martin left her cold. She didn't see Emery every day, but just the thought of her being down the hall, the idea that they worked at the same company kept their connection alive. She knew it was stupid, but it was the truth nonetheless. She and Emery had been nothing but complete professionals this entire time, both agreeing that what had happened was in the past, and the present was something very, very different. There was absolutely no chance of them getting back together. Hell, they weren't even *together* in the first place. It wasn't a relationship that had gone south; it was a fling. The mere definition of the word—a brief indulgence of your impulses—was exactly what it was. They had both used fake names, didn't share anything personal about each other except their bodies, and then it was over.

But this was very different. My God, it was like she had a teenage crush on Emery and wanted to "just be near her" twenty-four-seven. It had to stop. She was a professional and needed to stop thinking about Emery—what she was doing, who she was with at night. She needed to get on with her life. She needed a distraction, something to take her mind off Emery. A date, that's what she needed. She needed to get back out there into the dating world. She had a lot of friends, and how better to meet people than through other people? That was how she'd met the last few women she'd dated.

Dating seemed like such a passé word but what else would you call it? "Hooking up" was a euphemism for sex, and even though Dana had no problem hooking up when the circumstances were right, that wasn't exactly what she was looking for. However, maybe a good roll between the sheets would help her move past Emery.

Rocking the baby, Dana thought about that a little more. Along with the excitement of a new lover came the stumbling, awkwardness, and inevitable after-sex small talk. That she was not interested in. But if she wanted one, she would have to suffer through the other.

"Good God, Dana, suffer through? You make it sound so Victorian," she said out loud. She hadn't suffered through anything in a long time. Maybe that was also part of the problem. It had been months since the cruise. She missed being touched and definitely needed to release some pent-up energy. Seeing Emery so often didn't help. It was like a catch twenty-two. She needed to get her thoughts away from Emery yet she couldn't, or wouldn't. She was in a perpetual low-grade state of arousal that needed to bubble up and boil over, and soon.

Baby Grace started squirming in her arms and she chastised herself for letting her mind wander. She should be enjoying these first few minutes with this precious child, but as usual, she was thinking about her boss.

❖

"Do you know when she'll be back?" Emery asked. She hadn't seen Dana since yesterday morning. She had stopped by Dana's office this morning to talk about the upcoming board meeting, and Adam had told her Dana had left unexpectedly yesterday.

"I don't know. She got a phone call and ran out. She said it was personal." Adam had a puzzled look on his face. "I heard something about dilated or dilation or something like that," he added.

A thousand possibilities skittered around in Emery's head as to where Dana could have gone in such a hurry, but the main one was the very pregnant woman who had picked her up at the airport.

"She said she'd be back this morning. Then she called about eight thirty and asked me to clear her day and said she'd be in tomorrow instead. If you need something, Emery, I can call her cell. She said she could be reached anytime."

Other than the fact that she was curious about what had happened, this certainly wasn't an emergency. Dana had said it was personal, and unless it affected her job, it was none of Emery's business where she'd gone. She would have to wait until Dana returned to talk with her. She told Adam as much and returned to her office.

But she couldn't concentrate on work so she reached into her briefcase and pulled out a handful of papers and envelopes. Her mail had piled up in the last few weeks so she sifted through the pile, separating important from junk mail. Bills in one stack, she logged into her bank and practically on autopilot proceeded to direct the payments to and from the correct accounts. Her hand trembled as she looked at the return address on one specific envelope. It was the bill for her American Express card, taken care of by auto bill pay.

She hesitated before reaching for the letter opener. Her heart beat faster as the sharp blade sliced through the envelope like butter. Her hands shook as she held the paper that was folded in thirds.

She knew what she would see. This was more than the statement of her charges for the past four months. It was an itemized list of her charges from the cruise. She braced herself, which was ridiculous. It wasn't as if she had no idea of what the total would be or where the funds would come from. She never thought twice about how much she spent or on what. She was luckier than most to not have this worry, but she had worked hard to get to this point and wasn't going to feel guilty about it now. She gave generously to local charities and made sure Martin Engineering supported the community as well.

Between what she had inherited from her grandmother when she was twenty-two and her own savvy investment strategy, she had more money than most people realized. She found it refreshing and quite interesting when Dana refused to let her pay for things. When Dana had asked her if she'd like to go on a catamaran at their next port of call, Dana had flatly refused to accept Emery's money or let her pay for the excursion, simply stating, "No, I invited you." Simple as that.

They had slipped into a routine and both silently agreed that whoever asked, paid. So even though her American Express bill contained page after page of activities, she knew the same could be said for Dana's Visa statement.

There it was in black and white, line by line, recounting the most memorable experience of her life. Jet-ski rental in Half Moon Cay, parasailing in Grand Turk, dinner cruise in the Antilles, boat rental in the Dominican Republic, scuba-diving lessons in Bonaire, and rental fees for a private cabana in Martinique. The list went on and only reflected a partial list of their activities. These were the things she'd paid for. Dana's credit card certainly had similar details.

She wondered if Dana's heart beat a little faster when she looked at her bill. Did her thoughts turn into a highlight reel of the things they'd done together? Did she focus more on the time they'd spent together than the actual things they did? Did her hands tremble when she held her statement; did she close her eyes and inhale the remembered scent of each other?

Emery opened her eyes and shook her head. She was a mess. She'd known it wouldn't be easy having Dana so close, but she'd believed that in time the memories would fade and she and Dana would have a normal professional relationship.

She took off her glasses and rubbed her face with both hands. What a colossal misjudgment. Her emotions were just as much out of control today as they had been the first day she saw Dana in her office. She had completely underestimated the lingering effect Dana had on her and had absolutely no idea how to regain the steely control and focus she'd had over her life before she ever set eyes on Dana. Most unnerving was that she wasn't sure she wanted to.

❖

"Excuse me," Emery said instinctively after she ran into someone as she turned the corner. Papers scattered to the floor, and she looked into Dana's bright-green eyes.

"We need to install a traffic light," Dana replied, smiling.

"Or I need to watch where I'm going." Emery bent to pick up the papers that had fallen out of Dana's hands. She wasn't paying attention to where she was going, having been wondering for the past few days how she would ask Dana if her girlfriend had their baby. And now she was completely tongue-tied as she stared at Dana's silk-stocking-clad legs directly in front of her. Somehow she managed to rise but couldn't stop her eyes from traveling up Dana's body as she did. She felt a little dizzy.

"Are you okay?" Dana asked, frowning.

Hell no. "Of course. Here you go." She handed the papers to Dana.

"Thanks." Dana looked at her long and hard. "Are you sure you're okay?"

Emery realized she was staring and quickly answered, "Sure. I should ask you the same thing. Adam said you ran out of here pretty quickly the other day. Everything all right?" She hoped Dana would view her question as an opening to tell her what in the hell was going on.

Dana's expression shifted from concern to joy. "Yes, it's fabulous. I'm an aunt. Actually, an honorary aunt. My best friend and her partner had a baby on Tuesday. A little girl. Grace Foster Collier, five pounds, four ounces." She was practically beaming with pride, as if the child were her own.

A wave of relief flooded Emery when she realized she had jumped to the conclusion that the woman she saw Dana with at the airport was her girlfriend. She had been sickened at the thought that Dana would cheat and that she had played a part in it. Thank God that was over.

"Congratulations," she finally said. "Is it their first?" Her question sounded like she was being merely polite, but for some reason she felt that if it was important to Dana, it was important to her.

"Sort of. They've been foster parents for several years, but yes, this is their first. If Lauren has her way it'll be the first of many. Her partner, Elliott, on the other hand, is still a bit shell-shocked."

Dana's laugh filled the air around Emery. The sound was comforting and exciting at the same time. Dana laughed often in the office and her stomach fluttered every time she heard her. At times she even intentionally said something to Dana to produce that wonderful sound.

Dana looked at her watch. "I've gotta run," she said, already moving past Emery. "See you later."

She watched her hurry down the hall and paid special attention to make sure her mouth wasn't hanging open as Dana's hips swayed. Unlike most of the women who wore three-inch heels, Dana was graceful, her strides even and confident. Emery's mind flashed to a similar scene when Dana, this time naked, walked out of her bedroom to get something cold to drink. The muscles in her shoulders were well defined, the slope of her back perfect, the curve of her hips enticing. She had no control over her pulse as it increased its tempo.

She wasn't expecting Dana to look over her shoulder. Dana stopped, her eyebrows arched in surprise, then quickly lowered into a scowl. Quicker than when she walked away, Dana closed the space between them.

"Seriously? You're checking out my ass?" Her eyes flashed temper but her words remained quiet and calm. "Stop it, Emery," she added sternly before walking away again. This time she didn't turn around.

She bowed her head, closed her eyes, and pinched the bridge of her nose. She had to get ahold of herself. For the first time in her life her emotions were overriding her common sense. And that had never, ever happened in her professional life. How stupid and careless could she be? Anyone could have rounded the corner and seen the way she was ogling Dana. She wasn't concerned about what people thought of her, but she had risked Dana's reputation and that she would not do. She had promised herself and Dana that nothing would compromise her integrity.

Appropriately chastised, she returned to her office. As she sat behind her desk she didn't find the papers in front of her interesting. The blinking light signaling she had voice mail wasn't important. The forty-seven items in her in-box were suddenly not imperative.

She paced in front of the large window overlooking Mission Bay. She had rarely looked out this window with its view of the park and art museum. When she was in her office she was focused, dealing with the myriad issues, problems, and situations that only she had the answer to. She was drawn to her work, always scanning her e-mail, calling people, glad-handing and cultivating business associates.

Work was her life. It gave her meaning, a purpose, and she thrived on it.

But lately, she didn't feel the same zip, the same sense of excitement for what the day would bring. She was losing her patience more often, which had never happened before, and she found herself cutting off people if they didn't immediately get to the point.

Restless, instead of waking before her alarm she often hit the snooze button. Several times she actually overslept, her sleep patterns off due to her dreams of Dana—or, more accurately, Dee. For the first time in her life she felt as if she was missing something. But she was afraid to find out exactly what that something was.

Chapter Fourteen

Emery glanced up at the light knock on her door. Dana was standing in her doorway.

"You wanted to see me?"

Goddamnit, when was her heart going to stop jumping every time she saw Dana? "Yes, come on in, close the door."

Emery didn't get up from her chair behind her desk. Normally when she had people in her office, she directed them to the couch and chairs around the low table in the corner. It was a much more casual atmosphere and Emery liked the energy that was generated there. Sitting behind her desk signaled her link in the power chain, and she didn't like using it unless she absolutely had to.

But when Dana came into her office she did. She knew it was just a façade, but she needed this hunk of wood to help her maintain her professionalism, to keep her emotional distance from Dana. When she had staff meetings she always made sure Dana was sitting on the same side of the table so she wouldn't be as distracted. She made sure something or someone was between her and Dana and grudgingly admitted it was a complete waste of effort. Her body responded just when Dana stood on her threshold, let alone sat in front of her in a skirt with her legs crossed, exposing far, far too much skin for her to ever be able to concentrate.

She took several swallows of water from the bottle on the corner of the desk and made her brain focus. She glanced at her notes in front of her. Whenever she planned to have a one-on-one conversation with Dana she needed to take notes because her mind always turned to mush.

She was a successful executive of a multi-billion-dollar company who could do an off-the-cuff interview with *The Wall Street Journal*, give highly technical and complex speeches in front of thousands of people at conferences, and comfortably celebrate the birthday of the payroll clerk on the third floor. But when she was alone in a room with Dana, she turned into someone she had never known or would recognize as herself. She just wanted to listen to Dana talk, to hear her voice. Watch her hands move as she described something, watch her eyes light up when a thought or a concept energized her. Dana existed in her business life and Dee lived in her dreams.

"Emery?" Dana asked.

"Yeah…um…" She stumbled. She wanted to say, "I want you, Dana. To hell with the auditors, to hell with Martin and anybody or anything that gets in my way of having you again. I think about you all the time. I can't sleep without you next to me, I can't concentrate, I can't imagine my life without you." Instead she said, "Stephenson Electronics has proposed a merger."

"A merger? A company that's about ready to have the bank close their doors wants a merger with Martin? That's the kind of thinking that got them into the situation that they're in," Dana said dismissively.

"I know." Emery tried to get her mind back on track. "But this is a great deal. Their stock is worth pennies on the dollar. If we don't take them someone else will. And they have come to us. I've been talking with Phil Michaels, their CEO, and I think he'll agree that this would not be a merger. This is a straightforward acquisition. And now we need to make it happen."

"What do you want me to do?" Dana asked, opening her notebook and uncapping her Mont Blanc pen.

Kiss me, touch me, make love to me.

"I want you to lead this acquisition."

"Me?" Dana looked surprised.

Only you.

"I don't know what to say."

Just say yes.

"I'm flattered that you think I'm capable of handling this since I haven't been here that long."

"Yes, you." Emery replied confidently. "You are smart, have a good head on your shoulders, and know what questions to ask. You see the big picture and, most importantly, can get others to see it as clearly as you do. You hold people accountable and get things done. You're highly respected already and I think you can handle it."

Dana looked a bit shell-shocked but quickly recovered, and Emery could practically see her thinking through all the things she had to do.

"Excuse me, Emery," Adam said, sticking his head into the office. He turned his attention to Dana. "Dana, you wanted to know when Samuel Warrior called. He's on hold."

"Thanks, Adam," Dana said hesitantly, looking at Emery.

Emery waved her hand as if shooing Dana out the door. "Go ahead. We'll talk about this later."

"Thanks again, Emery, for your confidence." Dana stood and, with one last glance her way, hurried out the door.

Emery put her feet up on the desk and leaned back in her chair. She was tired. She'd had dinner at Julia's but ended up spending most of the evening thinking about Dana.

"Sit down, Emery. Your pacing back and forth is making me nauseous," Julia had said.

She'd stopped, realizing with a start that she was on the other side of Julia's living room. The last thing she remembered, they were finishing dinner in her kitchen. Julia had kicked off her sandals and tucked her model long legs under her on the couch.

"Sorry," she said sheepishly, quickly crossing the room and sitting in the overstuffed chair across from her BFF. "I guess I'm more keyed up than I thought."

"I'll say. You hardly said three things during dinner and you look like you're about to jump out of your skin."

"Sorry," she said again, leaning back and putting her feet up on the ottoman. She crossed her ankles and tried to focus. She felt bad. Julia's schedule was crazy yet she had carved out enough time to invite Emery over for dinner and to catch up on their lives, and she had responded by being a total space cadet.

"Spill it," Julia said without preamble, gathering her long brown hair up into a loose ponytail. "Something's obviously eating at you, and I'm not letting you out of here until you tell me what it is." When Emery didn't immediately answer, Julia fixed her dark eyes on her and asked, "Is it work? Some design that isn't working that you have to ride in and save the day and fix? An asshole government legislator breathing down your neck? Some newly discovered indiscretion you need to get your hands dirty cleaning up? Jeez, I thought you were done with those oozing out of the woodwork?" Julia spoke as if she had a mouth full of something distasteful.

Emery usually talked with Julia about the problems at Martin and about her personal life as well. Well, that was before she accepted the Martin job and actually *had* a personal life.

When she didn't immediately answer Julia asked, "Are you feeling okay?" Emery felt guilty for making her look so concerned. Even though Julia was a pediatrician, she had kept careful tabs on Emery when she was in the hospital. She had conferred with her doctors and helped her wade through all the medical jargon and options.

"I'm fine. Really, I'm feeling fine," Emery added when the concern remained after the first time she said it. "It's nothing like that." Julia had severely chastised her for ignoring her body's repeated messages to take care of herself.

"Then what is it? Something's obviously troubling you." Julia sat back looking like she could wait all night until Emery was ready to talk.

She didn't know where to start to describe the turmoil she was in. She had never felt like this. Always confident and sure of herself, she was now unsure, conflicted, on edge, anxious, and hesitant. The beginning was probably the best place, she decided. "Remember the woman I met on the cruise?"

"The one you called your cardiologist about asking if it was okay to have sex even though you were supposed to be resting? That woman?" Julia raised her eyebrows as if saying, "You devil, you."

"Yeah, that woman." Emery had called her doctor after the first evening with Dana. Somehow she had stumbled through asking if it was okay if she had sex. The last thing she wanted was to have a heart attack in some strange woman's cabin. Her doctor had cautioned her that unless she felt dizzy or light-headed or any of the other symptoms that had led her to the hospital in the first place, sex was okay. In fact he recommended it as a means of relaxation.

"Her name was Dee. Actually her name is Dana, and that's part of the problem." Julia remained quiet.

"We...uh...got together on the cruise...uh...quite a bit and she told me her name was Dee and I told her my name was EJ and we didn't say much of anything else about ourselves personally and to make a long story short, she now works for me." Emery finally took a breath.

"Run that by me again." Julia leaned forward in her chair.

"She works for me."

"No, the part about you hooked up, how did you phrase it, quite a bit?"

"Julia, that's not the problem," Emery stated firmly.

"We'll get to that later." Julia waved her hand as if to brush off that topic. "It's been so long since I've had sex I want to hear all about it. Every single detail."

"No, you don't.

"Yes, I do."

"No, you don't."

"Why not?"

"Because if it has been that long you couldn't handle it."

"Holy shit," Julia said, fanning herself with her hand. "Try me."

"Julia." Emery was exasperated. She appreciated Julia's attempt to lighten the mood, but she felt anything but jovial lately.

"Okay, we'll save that for two bottles of wine on the patio. Skip to the part about how she works for you."

Emery proceeded to lay out for Julia the chain of events that led up to her current state of confusion, even saying it sounded unbelievable how things had turned out the way they did.

"So, other than the obvious need for secrecy, what's the problem?" This time when Emery didn't answer, Julia filled in the silence. "Is she blackmailing you?"

"What? No, of course not." Surprisingly that thought had never crossed her mind.

"Then what is it?" Julia asked, seeming totally confused. Recognition then dawned on her face. "You've fallen for her!"

Emery winced. "Jeez, Julia, do you think you could've said it a little louder? I don't think your neighbor two doors down heard you clearly."

Julia looked appropriately scolded. "Sorry, but holy crap, Emery, you've never fallen for anybody."

"I have not fallen for her. It's just that…"

"It's just that you've fallen for her and you have no idea what to do about it."

Julia was partially right. She had had many relationships with women but none of them serious. The sex was always very good in the beginning but she grew bored quickly. That and her impossibly crazy work hours did little for building a relationship. But she had not fallen for Dana.

"I have not fallen for her," Emery repeated.

"Okay, I'll let that point drop for now. Tell me, what have you done?" Julia's eyes grew wide before she said, "You slept with her again!" This time Julia at least had the decency to whisper her last statement.

"For God's sake, Julia!" Emery's frustration came through and she barked at her. "You asked me a question about a hundred years ago, and if you would stop speculating and shut up I'll tell you." She took a couple of deep breaths to regain her composure.

"We're going to do an acquisition and I want Dana to be the project lead." That wasn't so hard, once Julia let her talk. She wasn't close to many people and worked very hard to maintain her image of always being in control and never doubting her own decisions. Julia was the only person she felt comfortable enough with to let her guard down.

"And that's a problem because…?"

"Because she's only been at Martin for a few months."

"And?"

"And she's never done an acquisition with us. She doesn't know our processes or systems.

"And?"

"And I'm not sure I'm thinking clearly," she finally admitted.

Julia frowned, her classic look as she concentrated on something. "So let me paraphrase what you just said. You're afraid to give her the job because you don't know if it's because you had sex with her, and we'll get back to that part of the conversation in a minute, or if you don't give it to her it's because you had sex with her and don't want to show her any favoritism. Is that it?"

"That's a mouthful but pretty much it."

Julia thought for a few moments. "Is she smart?"

"Very."

"Does she have experience with this kind of thing?"

"Yes."

"Does she know who to talk to and how to ask the right questions? Know where to go to get the answers?"

"Yes."

"Then what is the problem?"

Emery thought for a few minutes. Yes, Dana had never done an acquisition at Martin but that didn't mean she couldn't. Emery could help her through the unfamiliar aspects and then let her run with it. "I guess there isn't one."

A knock interrupted Emery's thoughts and Adam opened the door enough to stick his head in. "Excuse me, Emery. It's a little after three and the auditors are here. I put them in the conference room. Everybody is there."

Emery glanced at her watch. *Jesus Christ, Emery, get your head together.* "That's right. I'll be right there. Thanks, Adam."

Since the scandal at Martin Engineering the government auditors had taken claim to the entire fourth floor to review every conceivable record, piece of paper, and electronic file, and sometimes they sat in meetings to ensure that Martin was not engaging in any illegal or immoral activity.

On a quarterly basis they reported on their findings. The first several quarters were filled with dozens and dozens of examples of what could have very easily been simple errors of judgment or errors in calculations. However, with the trouble Martin was in, the auditors didn't view it that way.

When Emery came in as CEO she took a one-strike tolerance stance. This meant that every individual had one opportunity to make one mistake as long as it was in fact a mistake. The second incident of a similar nature and the individual was fired. It quickly became known that she would accept nothing less than for every Martin employee to conduct every transaction with as much honesty, professionalism, and accuracy as was humanly possible.

Every quarter the auditors' reports had fewer items of concern. Last quarter, the number was less than a dozen, and Emery had seen to it that those areas were addressed with the appropriate action immediately. This quarter she expected the number of incidents to continue to decrease.

She shook the day-dreaming cobwebs out of her head, grabbed her notes, and several minutes later entered the conference room. Sitting at the head of the table, which was her customary place for these meetings, she opened her notebook and glanced around the room. Her senior staff was there, including Dana, who was sitting next to the only female member of the audit team. The meeting went about as Emery had expected it would, and several members of her staff walked away with action items to follow up on discrepancies or questions the auditors had identified.

"Emery, you got a minute?" Steven, the lead auditor, asked after everyone had filed out of the room

"Sure, Steve. What's up?" Emery didn't begrudge the auditors what they did. They had a job to do, but it was her responsibility to see that these guys didn't have anything to do after a while at Martin Engineering.

"The auditor general just wanted to pass on his appreciation for the steps you've taken here. You've taken a good solid lead in dealing with the issues and getting this company back on the straight and narrow. One more quarter of results like this," he said, tapping the black folder, "well, I can't commit to anything, but if there are no other significant events, next quarter we just might be packing our boxes."

"Well, Steve," Emery said, extending her hand and shaking his. "Nothing personal but I'll be more than happy to help you pack."

After the meeting Emery stopped by Adam's desk. "Adam, Dana and I are going to head to Stephenson Electronics. We need to go to Singapore and Hong Kong."

"Okay," Adam replied, jotting notes on his green steno pad. "Is this an all-in-one trip?"

"Yes, it needs to be. I'm going to apologize right now and right up front because I know this will put my schedule in a complete turmoil and make your life a living hell. But we need to do this in the next three months."

"Three months!"

"I know, I know. I said I'm sorry."

"Don't worry about it, Boss. I'll work magic, I'll weave my charms, and I'll make this happen."

"Of that I have no doubt, Adam." Now if she just had the same confidence in herself. Traveling this long with Dana would be a challenge. A few months ago she would have laughed at any hint of being uncomfortable traveling with an employee. This trip would be something else altogether.

CHAPTER FIFTEEN

Dana was nervous as she opened the door. She gave her name to the maître d' and followed him through the restaurant toward the back of the large room. Couples and foursomes sat in intimate settings around tables draped with white tablecloths, candles, and sparkling flatware. Low music played in the background from a three-piece combo in the corner. The lights were low and no one paid her any attention, which put her more on alert. The thick carpet under her feet muffled any sound as they approached the table.

"Thank you, John, another glass of wine for me, and Dana, what would you like?"

"Iced tea please, with lemon." Dana had no idea what this dinner was about and she fully intended to stay completely sober.

"Thanks for meeting with me, Dana. I just wanted to take some time, off the record so to speak, and see how you're settling in at Martin."

"Things are going really well. Thank you for asking," she replied carefully. When the call came on her home phone from Sharon Plenner, one of Martin's board members, she was puzzled, to say the least. General conversation at the office was one thing, but a rendezvous that she had been asked to keep to herself was something altogether different. She wasn't sure what to wear to this dinner so she settled on business attire. Her trousers were black, her blouse white silk, her jacket red.

"Good, good. The first few months can be hard. Getting to know everyone, the ins and outs of the company, who the players and the receivers are," Sharon stated, finishing the wine remaining in her glass.

"It can be, yes, but everyone at Martin has made me feel very welcome."

"That's nice to hear." Sharon opened her menu. "The duck here is very good, as is the crab. They fly it in from Alaska daily."

Dana turned the page on her menu and glanced at the entrées. She wasn't really hungry, her stomach unsettled. She wasn't normally nervous meeting with higher levels of management or senior politicos. In her line of work she often rubbed elbows with the powerful. This, however, was the first time the scene had been in a discreet restaurant and obviously off the record.

Their order placed, Dana commented on the décor. It resembled that of a quaint bistro in Italy she had stumbled on in an out-of-the-way street in Florence.

"It's my favorite place to come when I want to have a conversation and not have dozens of people overhear me." Sharon looked Dana in the eye, her message clear.

Dana was now even more suspicious than she was when she walked in. Something was going on. A board member didn't invite her to dinner and ask her to keep it between the two of them to simply talk about her transition.

"What can I do for you, Mrs. Plenner?" Dana didn't like the way the conversation was going already.

"Dana, please call me Sharon."

Dana froze when Sharon reached across the table and touched the top of her hand. *What the fuck?* Sharon was well into her sixties and unattractively thin. Her hair was dyed jet-black and her face pulled way too tight. She wore gaudy diamond rings on her left hand and an equally ostentatious ruby on the right. Matching earrings dangled from her drooping earlobes.

Sharon removed her hand. "Let's enjoy our dinner before we talk shop, shall we?"

Dana managed to choke down her meal, needing large amounts of tea to get it past her dry throat. Her throat was dry and her stomach threatened to reject everything she put in it. Sharon dominated the conversation and they discussed everything from the symphony to the new president of North Korea. Dana couldn't afford to let her guard slip no matter how innocuous the topics were.

Their waiter cleared their dishes and offered coffee. Sharon declined in favor of her fourth glass of wine and Dana ordered decaf. Dana didn't say anything. She wasn't going to continue to make small talk with Sharon. The evening was completely bizarre and Dana was anxious to get out of here.

"Emery is an interesting individual, isn't she?" Sharon said.

Dana kept quiet. She didn't know what Sharon was fishing for, but she refused to offer anything.

"Do you know much about her?"

"I did quite a bit of research on Martin before I decided to apply. Some of it included Emery."

"Do you know much about her personally?"

"Not much, no."

"She's dedicated to her work."

"I think at her level it's certainly more than a full-time job," Dana replied diplomatically.

"Do you know she had to take some time off recently to...uh... how shall I put this...rest?"

Sharon's emphasis on the word *rest* implied something much more than its definition. She made it sound secretive and just a bit tawdry. Anyone listening could interpret it to be anything from a nervous breakdown to a stint in rehab.

"I wasn't aware of that, and I don't think it's any of my business what she does with her time."

"She said she went on a cruise." Sharon's tone said she didn't believe it.

"Yes, I had heard that too. It was right before my final set of interviews. That was why I had to wait a few weeks before I was able to meet with her." Dana defended Emery as best she could at this point.

"Has she talked about the cruise? Where she went, the cruise line, the other people on the ship, who she went with?"

Is that what this is about? "I'm not certain exactly where she went. I heard her answer some questions about a cruise but nothing more." Dana didn't reply to the other three questions.

"And she hasn't talked to you about it?"

"Why would she?" Dana finally got her own question in.

"Isn't that what people do when they come back from a trip? Show pictures, talk about it, brag about the fish that got away?" Sharon said, wrinkling her nose and obviously disgusted at the thought.

"I suppose some do but some don't as well." Dana sipped her coffee and the waiter discreetly laid the bill on the edge of the table between them. She was getting tired of this cat-and-mouse game. "Are you trying to determine something?"

"No," Sharon replied, a little too quickly. "If there's something I need to know I'll just ask. I'm just curious, that's all."

Dana wanted to say, "Then why aren't you asking Emery these questions," but knew not to.

Sharon took another healthy swallow of her wine. "It's tough to be the only woman on a board made up exclusively of sixty-year-old white men."

Did she just say that?

"We're in the second decade of the new millennium and it's still so much the old boys' club. Conversations and deals made on the golf course and at the urinal."

Dana almost choked on her coffee. She managed to cover her reaction with a small cough instead. She doubted that Sharon even noticed. Her eyes were glassy and she was starting to slur her words.

"What I'm looking for, Dana, is a partner, an ally, a confidante, if you will. Someone to help keep Martin on the right track."

"And you think I'm that person?"

"Yes, I do." Sharon laid her clammy hand on Dana's again. "I think you are the perfect person."

I didn't like this meeting in the first place and I definitely don't like it now.

"What about Emery? As the CEO isn't she the most logical choice to keep Martin on the right track?" Dana asked, using the phrase Sharon just used.

"Yes, she is, against my vote by the way, which obviously doesn't mean anything to those men. Those old fools think the sun rises and sets on her. She can do no wrong in their eyes."

Dana slowly removed her hand from under Sharon's. She would have to be very careful here. She had a lot of experience thwarting unwanted advances from both men and women, but this was a first. If she made an enemy of Sharon it would not bode well for her, Emery, or Martin. "Sharon, I'm uncomfortable with this conversation. I don't think you should be talking to me about board matters."

"Bullshit. I can talk to whomever I want whenever I want." Sharon practically spat the words. "Now what about my proposition?"

"I'm flattered, Sharon, but I don't think I can help you."

"I know you can," Sharon said again, setting her glass on the table a little too hard. The wine spilled onto the pristine white cloth.

Dana reached into her purse and withdrew three twenty-dollar bills. She placed them inside the black folder that held their bill. "No, Sharon, I won't. I have to go now. Please take care."

Dana left the table before Sharon could call her back and quickly crossed the large room. She stopped at the maître d's booth just long enough to ask that they call Sharon a cab and hurried out the front door. Once outside she picked up her pace across the parking lot. She started her car and didn't breathe again until she was out of the lot.

She drove home completely stunned. She had been around the block more than a few times in the business world, but she had never had someone offer a proposal like the one Sharon Plenner had. She wasn't even sure exactly what the proposition was. On one hand she could have interpreted it as sexual, but on the other it was more like she wanted Dana to be her spy. Either way she was very uncomfortable with the position Sharon had put her in.

Several things troubled her about the entire evening. First was the subterfuge, and second was the amount of liquor Sharon had put away, especially because she didn't appear to be concerned when she clearly had too much. Then there was her support, or lack thereof, of Emery as Martin's CEO. Sharon apparently didn't support Emery and had admitted that she had voted against her. Even now after everything Emery had done to turn Martin around, Sharon was still against her. It was pretty evident that she was looking for dirt, especially as it related to Emery.

Dana wondered how many people Sharon had approached with her proposal. There were two other women on Emery's staff: Joanne

Fister, the head of legal, and Consuela Marquez, the head of their operations in Latin America. Had Sharon had a similar conversation with them? If so, had she been successful in recruiting them to be her mole? Was she the only one Sharon had approached and was it because she was a lesbian? No one would even suspect Sharon was anything other than a shrewd businesswoman, and a straight one at that. She touted her role as wife, mother, grandmother, and community philanthropist. Dana's gaydar never flickered when she first met Sharon, and it certainly hadn't this evening.

Sharon had asked that Dana keep their dinner just between the two of them. She found that odd, and even though she'd agreed to it, she would make her own decision as to whether she would talk to Emery about it. Something was definitely going on, and until she knew more she didn't plan to say anything.

She drove aimlessly through the city for another hour before she went home. Dozens of questions bounced around in her head, and she relived several meetings where, if Sharon had been successful, negative information could have gotten back to her. Sharon had not alluded to knowing anything. On the contrary, she was on a fishing expedition and wanted Dana as her bait.

Dana knew she wouldn't sleep well tonight so didn't even try. She sat on the chaise lounge on her patio, the night still warm enough to sit outside. She loved her backyard. Tall trees surrounded a large deck, and accent lighting softened the darkness. As she relaxed, her thoughts drifted.

"We'll be docking in Nassau in the morning."

"Mm-huh," EJ replied behind her. They were sitting on a lounge chair on the veranda, Dee between EJ's long legs, leaning back against her. A soft, warm breeze ruffled her hair and EJ smoothed it down with one hand, then returned both arms around her middle. They had been sitting like this for a while, a light blanket covering their naked bodies.

Dee had ventured out here while EJ slept after another round of torrid, exciting sex. She couldn't seem to get enough of EJ. Not that EJ was complaining; she too seemed to be insatiable.

Sex was not the only thing that held them together. Just this evening she and EJ had had dinner with Vivian and Rose, the four of them talking about current events, activities, and excursions they had gone on, and even some general ship gossip, like old friends. EJ held her hand while they strolled across the main deck and they seemed to naturally navigate back to EJ's suite.

"Did you make any plans for Nassau? The Bahamas has some of the clearest water in the world for snorkeling."

"Nope," EJ answered, nuzzling her neck.

"Nothing?" Dee asked. "You can go jet skiing, parasailing, kayaking, on a glass-bottom boat, biking around the island." She rattled off the list of activities available when they arrived in port. She knew there were several more, but EJ's lips on her throat and her hands on her breasts made it difficult to think, let alone remember.

"Not interested." EJ's hands began to move with more interest over her breasts, tweaking her nipples between her thumb and fingers. It hadn't taken EJ long to discover that there was a direct circuit from her nipples to her clit, and she exploited it to the fullest. Dee arched her back for more, starting to move her legs back and forth on the wide chair.

"You don't want to do any of the activities?" Dee managed to choke out, not sure why she was asking.

EJ removed one hand and slowly slid it down her stomach. She inhaled sharply at the seductive movement, causing her breast to fill EJ's hand even more. Knowing full well its intended location, Dee breathed in quick, anticipating gasps.

"Nope, I'd rather stay here and do this. All that other stuff—been there, done that," EJ said. Her fingers inched lower, agonizingly slow, and her tongue slid around the outside of Dee's right ear.

She managed to catch her breath for a moment. "Can't you say the same about what you're doing now?" She was struggling to maintain a coherent conversation with EJ when her fingers were dancing over her body. She loved talking with EJ, trading barbs and wit and teasing, seductive comments and innuendos. Combining sex and casual conversation was downright arousing, hot and just a bit naughty. Kind of like pretending nothing was going on when *everything* was going on.

EJ's breath was warm in her ear and she felt her smile. "Not hardly. I want to discover so much more about you."

She grabbed the arms of the chair and gasped as EJ ran her fingers lightly over her clit. She strained into the touch, needing more than teasing flicks across the sensitive point. "Oh, God, EJ." She moaned loud enough that the neighbors could hear if they were outside. She had stopped caring about that at EJ's first touch.

EJ was hot behind her, rubbing her pubic mound against her ass as much as she could in such tight quarters. She needed to come but needed to touch EJ more. She slid her hand between them, directly into EJ's warmth. EJ shuddered against her back, her wetness filling her hand.

"Oh, Jesus." Now EJ moaned, into her hair, her own breathing ragged. "God, this feels good. I can't get enough of you."

EJ lightly bit the place where her neck curved into her shoulder. She moaned even louder this time. EJ's fingers were in her, her nipple was sending electric jolts to the center of her universe, and EJ was hot in her hand. What more was there?

"Shh, the neighbors will hear you," EJ said, surprising her.

"At this point I don't give a fuck who hears me," she croaked out, her throat raw with desire. Her body was on fire, and she was seconds from exploding under the stars in her lover's skillful arms. But she needed one thing more. She let go of her death grip on the chair arm and touched herself. She stifled a groan, on the verge of climax.

"Speaking of fucking," she said, and increased the speed of both hands. She felt EJ's sex in her hand, under her fingers, and what EJ did with one hand she did with the other. Bringing herself and EJ to climax the same way was exquisite. Her vision blurred.

EJ realized what she was doing and quickened her own pace. "God, Dee, yes."

She couldn't hold back any longer, nor did she want to. "Fuck me, EJ!"

Dana staggered off the patio and into her bed, the cool sheets warming under her hot body. Her hands retraced the intimate encounter as she screamed into the darkness. "Fuck me, Emery!"

CHAPTER SIXTEEN

"One last thing," Emery said before her staff meeting ended a few weeks later. "Adam will be sending each of you your invitation to the annual holiday get-together. The usual suspects, members of the board and some key customers, and a few others. My house, as usual, Saturday, December first, sevenish. Everyone is a plus one." She looked around the table, saving Dana for last. "Just give Adam your RSVP by Thanksgiving."

"Jack, are you going fishing over Christmas again this year?" the man to Emery's left asked as she gathered up her papers. Emery saw Dana's eyes darken.

EJ found Dee standing in line at the concierge desk. She had been looking for her everywhere after discovering her side of the bed empty. She missed waking up with Dee in her arms, and that surprised her. Normally she was the one to get up and go home before dawn, or if the woman was at her house she was up, showered, and dressed before she woke. It was a clear signal that the encounter was over and they were to each go their own way. However, waking with Dee was nice.

Dee wore khaki cargo shorts, a blue tank top, and tennis shoes. A pair of black sunglasses was perched on top of the brim of a white cap. She was, in a word, hot. She looked fit and very athletic, and EJ suspected she was capable of doing just about anything she set her mind to. The woman behind Dee started making conversation with her, and even though EJ was too far away to hear what they were saying, her movements said they were talking about the brochure in Dee's hands.

EJ inhaled sharply and felt what could only be described as a pang of jealousy. WTF? She had never been jealous and had absolutely no reason to start now. She and Dee had agreed to a cruise fling, and to EJ that meant just the two of them, also known as exclusivity. What if Dee didn't think the same? Would EJ end the fling? She didn't like to share and was going to have to decide what to do if Dee did.

She was debating her next move when a stunning redhead in a too-tight shirt and way-too-short shorts sidled up next to the woman talking to Dee. She put her arm around her and planted what looked like a very sloppy, intimate kiss on her mouth. Dee turned away politely and returned to reading her brochure. EJ breathed again when she realized the woman no longer was a threat. How childish was that, she thought as she walked over to where Dee stood.

"Plans for the day?" she asked over Dee's left shoulder. Dee leaned back into her, the touch of their bodies sending a spark of desire through her. She lifted her hands and placed them on Dee's waist. The pamphlet shook slightly in Dee's hands.

"As a matter of fact, I have reservations to go fishing."

"Fishing? As in guts-on-a-hook fishing?" she asked, surprised.

"Is there any other kind?" Dee replied.

"I suppose not, at least not in this context. Do you fish?" Somehow they both had stayed away from personal questions, but she didn't think this fell into that line of questions. And she wanted to know.

"As often as I can," Dana replied. "Do you?"

"I've been a time or two but never in open water. I just never had the opportunity."

The line moved closer to the desk as the women ahead of them received the information they needed from the concierge. EJ's crotch throbbed at the rubbing of their bodies together as they moved a few steps forward. She wanted to toss the brochure into the nearest trash and drag Dee back to her cabin. She smiled at the thought.

"What are you smiling about?" Dee asked, turning her head slightly and giving EJ access to her neck, which she immediately took advantage of.

"How much I'd like to drag you back to my cabin, but if I remember correctly you would probably beat me there." She nibbled on the soft skin below Dee's left ear. Dee shuddered against her then stepped away.

"You're right, I probably would," Dee said with a seductive smile that sent her pulse into overdrive. But we have all night and all day tomorrow for that, and today I'm going fishing."

Dee was right. The ship would be leaving at seven thirty this evening and sail for the next thirty-six hours until they arrived in Bonaire.

"I must be losing my touch," she said, teasing.

Dee stepped closer and pressed a much-too-quick kiss on her lips. "Trust me, Ms. Connor. I find your touch nothing less than spectacular. But don't tempt me. I want to go fishing," Dee said again.

She lifted her hands in surrender. "Okay, okay, you win. I'll leave you alone. For now," she added for clarification. "Mind if I just keep you company?"

"As long as that's all you do, just keep me company." Dee pointed at her. "No smooth words, passionate looks, nibbles, or touches. I mean it." Dee was trying to sound serious.

It thrilled her to know that Dee was as affected by their time together as she was. From what she'd said it wouldn't take much persuasion to get her right back in bed, or on the counter, the couch, or up against the wall with her fingers buried inside her. She exhaled deeply. She needed to stop thinking like this or it would be a long day. A very long day.

"I'll behave," she said. When it was Dee's turn at the counter EJ said, "I'll give you some privacy. I'm going to get a paper. Meet me over there?" She pointed to a large fountain not far from where they stood.

EJ sat on the bench across from the fountain and was reading the front page when something dropped in her lap. She looked up and Dee was standing in front of her, with a mischievous grin. She picked up the envelope. "What's this?"

"Open it and find out."

She opened the flap and a ticket fell into her hands.

"I thought you might like to go."

She looked up at Dee, surprised. "This is a ticket," she said, immediately feeling stupid for stating the obvious.

"I don't know what you do for a living, EJ, and I don't want to know, but you must be somebody important because you're pretty smart."

Her heart jumped this time, due to Dee's reference to her job. What if she did know who she was? Would it make a difference? Would she be attracted to the power she had as the CEO of a Fortune 1000 company? Would she find it sexy and a turn-on to bed her? Would she be like the others?

"EJ?"

Dee was standing in front of her looking worried. "Sorry, I'd love to go. Thanks for thinking of me." She pulled herself out of her five-second funk. She stood up and kissed Dee. "You know, I wasn't *fishing* for an invitation," she said, raising her eyebrows à la Groucho Marx. She was rewarded by Dee's smile.

"That's good because this is a catch-and-release trip." Dee paused. "You know, bait the hook, the fish strikes, enjoy the thrill of catching it, take a few pictures to memorialize the adventure, then let it go." Dee paused again. "Seems to fit, doesn't it?"

Dee held her eyes for several seconds. Her analogy was crystal clear. That was exactly what they were doing with their cruise fling. This was Dee restating their agreement after hours of sex, and EJ's opportunity to do the same. She didn't know why she was hesitating. That was exactly what she wanted, and she'd brought it up in the first place. She was in no place to and had no desire to have anything other than an uncomplicated, undemanding affair. They were only a few days into the cruise, and in less than three weeks, she'd be back at her desk with no time for any distractions. So why hadn't she readily agreed?

Dee must have taken her silence for agreement because she said, "The launch leaves in an hour and you've got to get ready."

EJ had never been on a fishing boat large enough to hold ten other anglers. Rob, the captain, made everyone feel welcome and comfortable as soon as they got on board. The safety demonstration over, they were fitted with their rods and he turned the boat into the open water.

It wasn't long before Dee had a hit. She settled into the specially made chair, buckled herself in, and put her feet on the blocks. According to Captain Rob it could take several hours or more of reeling and maneuvering the big fish until it was close enough to be netted and brought into the boat.

EJ watched Dee, completely spellbound by her physical strength. She had been in the chair for over two hours and was covered with sweat. Her arms were tan from the sun, the muscles standing out from the strain of fighting the fish. The way she rocked the long pole back and forth and spun the reel was smooth and sensuous. Even though her hair was in a ponytail pulled through the back of the cap, several strands had escaped and were blowing in the breeze. Her sunglasses that had hidden her eyes from EJ's view were on her red nose. Her face was set in concentration and determination; she was completely focused. Finally the fish was in the net and the two deck hands were hoisting it aboard.

"Holy shit," Dee said. The exhaustion in her voice contrasted sharply with the look of radiance on her face.

EJ caught her breath when she looked at Dee. She was tired, the signs apparent at the way her arms hung limply at her sides, but she looked like she could go another hour with the big fish. The look of accomplishment on her face was breathtaking.

"It's got to be at least six feet long," Dee said excitedly as the deck hand reached for his tape measure. "It's an Atlantic blue marlin."

"My God, it's beautiful," she said, both about the fish and Dee. It had been exciting watching Dee alternately fight and finesse the fish until it gave up the battle. It was one of the most exciting, arousing things she had ever witnessed.

"Six feet, eight inches," the deck hand said in a harsh accent.

"Wow," Dee said, clearly amazed.

"Let's get a couple of pictures before we toss him back," Captain Rob said.

EJ handed him Dee's camera and took several pictures with her own as well. These pictures might be the only ones she would have of Dee, and they would reflect her personality, guts, and beauty all in one shot.

❖

Emery's house was stunning. It wasn't the largest on the block, far from it, but the subtle, unpretentious design made it warm and inviting. As Dana followed the directions that came with her invitation she estimated the houses in the neighborhood had to be at least six or seven thousand square feet, if not substantially more. Each was on what looked like an acre, the lawns lush and meticulously landscaped even at this time of the year.

The valet opened her door and offered his hand to help her out. She thanked him, as it was difficult to maneuver in and out of her low-slung Lexus in the dress she had finally decided to wear tonight. He was polite enough not to ogle her legs as she slid out of the driver's seat, but the way he clenched his jaw showed it was work. She reminded herself to give him a generous tip for his professionalism.

The door opened a few seconds after she rang the bell, her hands moist with perspiration. She was nervous and for an instant had debated whether to even come. But unless she was desperately ill, not attending was not an option.

Adam surprised her by opening the door. He took her wrap and purse and passed them off to a waiting woman, who disappeared into the room next to the foyer.

"Dana, you look sensational," he said, lightly holding her wrists and lifting her arms out to her sides. "That dress is gorgeous and I shouldn't say this but I can because I'm a gay guy and there is nothing remotely sexual in my comment but you look absolutely stunning." Adam said all that in one big breath.

She had debated for hours whether to shop for a new dress for the party. She had several that would have been more than appropriate for the professional/personal gathering this evening obviously was. She could have worn her blue Vera Wang or her classic Chanel, but Lauren had insisted she buy something "stunning, yet professional."

She had chosen a black V-neck wrap dress from Anne Klein's fall collection. Made of a blended wool-and-spandex fabric, the simple, yet elegant lines complemented her shape without being provocative. The dress had a high neckline in the back, capped sleeves, and wrapped around like a robe, but the strategic ties and snaps, and the alligator belt with a brilliant silver buckle at her waist, held it all together. The front was cut low enough to be attractive but didn't show any cleavage. This was a business gathering, after all. Her classic black patent-leather pumps had a slightly higher heel than what she wore at the office. The hemline separated in the front, curving slightly upward. All in all a very classic, elegant look.

"Thank you. You look quite handsome yourself in your tuxedo. Armani?" she asked.

"Is there any other?" Adam took her arm and led her into the room to where the other guests were mingling. She glanced around the room and saw many of her coworkers, familiar faces she recognized, and a few complete strangers. Everyone was in their festive best, with diamonds and black tie abundant.

Adam excused himself to answer the door again and Dana accepted a glass of wine from the waiter. As she sipped the warm liquid she immediately spotted Emery talking with a group of white-haired men, one of which was the senior senator from Maine. Emery was animated and friendly with the men, completely at ease with Senator Marshall, one of the most powerful men in the country. Marshall controlled the defense-budget's purse strings and ultimately Martin Engineering contracts.

At first Dana wondered if there was any conflict-of-interest issue with Senator Marshall attending the Martin Engineering holiday gathering. His attendance as well as the presence of the several other congressmen and senators Dana recognized could be misconstrued. But she trusted Emery's judgment, as well as the fact that three of the government auditors that had offices down the hall from hers were standing by the fireplace keeping an eye on everyone.

Her casual perusal of the room was interrupted when someone to her left said, "Dana, good to see you." It was Jack and a woman she guessed was his wife.

"Jack, good to see you too tonight," she replied politely. She hated small talk but had gotten pretty good at it, enough to survive.

He introduced his wife, who said with an appreciative glance, "I love your dress."

"Thank you, yours as well," Dana said, more from habit than actually liking the red sequined dress on the overly large woman. She commented on Jack's tuxedo. "Jack, you clean up pretty good."

"I hate these things," he replied, tugging on his too-tight collar. It was definitely a last-year-and-twenty-pounds-ago shirt. "Thank God, Emery is more prone to khakis than formal at the office." He chuckled a little before adding, "I sure am glad I'm not intimidated, because Emery looks better in her tuxedo than most of the men in this room."

She had to agree and remembered the first time she saw Emery looking as strikingly attractive as she did tonight.

The event was the captain's dinner, the invitation specifying the evening wear as black tie. However, EJ's was royal blue, accentuating her deep-olive complexion. When Dee had opened her cabin door to EJ's knock she was stunned by how handsome EJ was in formal wear.

Tonight was no exception. Instinctively Dana knew it was the same suit and she flushed all over when she remembered unbuttoning the vest and everything underneath it.

Emery had almost exhausted the suitable topics for conversation when Adam rescued her. "Excuse me, Ms. Barrett, but another guest has arrived. She's talking to Jack and his wife."

She already knew it was Dana, without turning around. She seemed to instinctively know where Dana was whenever she was close and feel her hollow absence when she wasn't. She held her breath to see if Dana had in fact brought a "plus one."

She remained cautiously optimistic when she saw that Dana was alone. Her date could be anywhere, but as she approached Dana she didn't care.

Dana looked stunning in her dress, the neckline not low enough to be inappropriate but too high for what she wanted to see on Dana. Her hair was up in a classic French braid, giving her an aura of elegant sophistication. Her hair, dress, and makeup were perfect, and she couldn't take her eyes off her as she approached.

"Dana, thank you for coming." Her voice cracked. Her throat was dry, her hands were shaking, and the rest of her body was going haywire as well.

"I told her it was an annual event that people anticipated for weeks and talked about for months." Jack's comments jarred Emery back to the reality that she and Dana were not alone in this big room.

"Tell Adam, it's his thing. I just sign the check," she said, more casually than she felt. She had to work hard to keep her eyes from drifting to the vee in Dana's dress or at the slit in the front. She absolutely could not do that here with these people.

"Then I'll thank you for the invitation and him for how much I'm enjoying myself," Dana said lightly. "Nice suit," Dana said, looking at her before turning her attention back to the others. "Jack, you forgot to add that in addition to looking quite dapper tonight, Emery is extremely humble as well."

She couldn't breathe. Those were the exact words Dana had used to compliment her at the captain's dinner. And she remembered exactly how her body had trembled in anticipation as Dana slowly removed her clothes. Emery couldn't help but touch a button on the vest, her nerves a mess. Her eyes met Dana's and she knew Dana remembered too. Her knees threatened to collapse and she was slow to respond.

"Yeah, well, enough of the flattery contest. I have guests to attend to, and you have food to eat and alcohol to drink." Somehow she was able to step away. "Please, everyone, enjoy yourself. I'll catch up with you all later."

She had an almost-full glass of wine in her hand and finished it in one swallow. She knew she shouldn't drink that fast, but she needed something to smack some sense into her. With Dana looking like that and her memories intruding in this important night, it would be a long night indeed.

❖

"Okay, everyone, time for the grand tour. For those of you that haven't been, it starts in five minutes. Five minutes, everyone get your tickets," Adam said, pretending he was a barker at a carnival.

Even though Dana was curious about where Emery lived, she certainly didn't want her to know. She had no intention of peering into every room. She would simply walk around the rooms where the party was going on and gather as much intel as she could that way.

She wanted to know everything about Emery. Her likes, dislikes, what chair she sat in to watch TV, how she lined up her clothes in her closet. God, she sounded like a stalker—or a teenager with a big crush. She struggled not to cross that line every day. She wasn't about to make that thread any thinner by tempting fate. And walking through the rooms that Emery occupied, seeing her things, feeling her presence in her home would be a temptation she didn't know if she was strong enough to resist.

"Come on, Dana, let's go," Adam called from his perch on the third step of the staircase.

"No, that's okay. I'll just hang out here."

"Nonsense," Adam said, waving his hand in her direction. "You cannot miss this. Come on, everyone takes the tour. It's a company requirement."

She knew he was just kidding, but judging by the people gathered around Adam, they thought it was.

"Emery's house is legend," he added for emphasis.

Dana hesitated, knowing that if she continued to refuse she would cause suspicion and talk. Or so she said to convince herself.

Adam led the eager group through the rooms downstairs. And as he did he explained about the construction and the ecological design of the house, and even through the technical jargon, she saw traces of Emery's personality throughout. A sculpture here, a painting there, a couple of knickknacks above the fireplace in the living room were subtle signs of what made Emery tick.

Everyone had naturally gathered in the living room of the large house. From the outside, she would never have thought it was as large as it was inside. The ceilings were high, and the absence of walls gave the space an open and inviting feeling. Polished wood floors reflected the overhead lights, giving the room an unusual sensation of warmth.

Several large pieces of comfortable-looking furniture filled the room but didn't dominate the space. It looked lived in, a place where friends could gather and watch football on the sixty-inch television or simply enjoy a bottle of good wine and catch up.

Dana, no connoisseur in the kitchen, knew enough to recognize that the appliances were top-of-the-line, the countertops crushed granite, the cabinets real hardwood. A few quirky things stood out, like an almost-antique coffee pot and equally old toaster, and a Norman Rockwell painting of a large family gathered around the dinner table.

Adam quickly passed through the remaining rooms on the first floor, chattering practically nonstop. Entering Emery's office, most of her fellow guests, or what Dana thought of them as *house voyeurs*, gave the room nothing but a polite glance. Dana, however, was very interested in it. Emery conducted business here. As a successful professional Dana was always curious about where people worked, how they worked, what kind of things they did to successfully stay on top of their profession and the competition.

Emery's office was a lot like hers with the requisite desk, credenza, computer, printer, and assorted paperwork. Her bookshelves, however, were quite surprising and, other than the familiar business books, contained a variety of literature, fiction from the latest popular authors, and a few reference books.

Dana was alone in the room, the other tourists having moved on ahead of her. She walked behind Emery's desk, inhaling the scent of the leather from her chair. She ran her finger over the top of the fine cherrywood of the desk. She fingered the paperclips, touched the stapler, and lightly ran her fingers over the keyboard. She imaged Emery sitting here, her Bluetooth stuck in her ear, having a conversation with the production manager in Hong Kong, the quality-assurance director in Thailand, or giving Adam instructions.

A picture on the desk caught her attention and she reached for it. Its heavy frame was a perfect match for the photo inside. Her heart stopped and she quickly looked around to verify that she was still alone. She remembered precisely when the photo was taken, and she had one exactly like it. Their scuba instructor had taken it off the coast of Bonaire. He had captured the intimate image of her and Emery perfectly as they saw a giant stingray for the first time.

They both had spotted the stingray sweep by so close they could almost touch it. She remembered the wonder of seeing such a beautiful creature. Its graceful, long, languid movements were awe-inspiring. Emery had felt it too, and they had talked about it after they went ashore. She remembered the look of excitement in Emery's eyes as she described it.

Thick masks and large regulators made the two divers unrecognizable to anyone who didn't know who they were, but she did. More importantly, Emery did as well. She returned the picture to the place of prominence on the desk, and with one last look around, her legs shaking, she went to find the rest of the tour.

"Dana, there you are. I thought we'd lost you," Adam said, waving her toward another open door. She froze when she heard a familiar clack.

Chapter Seventeen

Pool? You want to play pool?"

"Yes, there's a table on the Sports deck. Can I interest you in a game?"

"I don't know how to play. I mean I know the balls are hit into the pockets, but that's about it," Dee said, somewhat skeptical. "I've seen it played but don't know the rules or anything."

"I'll teach you."

EJ held out her hand in invitation. She had tingled inside when she saw EJ walking toward her. "Come on, it'll be fun. I promise." Fun, amusement, and a little something she didn't recognize glinted in EJ's dark eyes.

"As long as you don't let me win," she said, putting her hand in EJ's. "I hate it when people do that."

"I promise." EJ crossed her heart with her free hand. "You will win only if you beat me fair and square."

"Now you're teasing me," she said as they arrived at the stairwell to the next deck. EJ stopped and motioned for her to go first.

She had to let go of EJ's hand, and as she did EJ stepped close to her and whispered, "No, that comes later," and followed her up the steps. The billiards room was located at the stern of the Sports deck adjacent to the video arcade.

EJ reclaimed her hand as they continued across the deck toward the billiards room. The heat of EJ's hand in hers traveled up her arm, through her body, and found a cozy home in the pit of her stomach. Every time EJ touched her, she felt it like a hot poker followed by warm water cascading over her skin.

"God, I love warm weather," she said, raising her eyebrows as they passed several scantily clad women sunbathing on deck. A few more were lying on rafts in the pool, and a waitress in short shorts and a tank top bearing the Seafair logo over her rather large breasts carried a tray full of drinks.

"I'm speechless," EJ said, and winced when she playfully slapped her arm.

"Hey!"

"If you hope to continue experiencing wild and passionate with me, you better think of something to say. And it better be the right thing. I don't share."

EJ looked at her, in her own pair of shorts and a scoop-neck T-shirt. "I prefer the mystery of discovering what's underneath rather than too much exposed?" EJ said, her eyebrows arched as if asking a question.

"Good answer."

"Thank you. Now, let me give you a crash course in the finer elements of pool," EJ said as they entered the room.

The space was decorated like a traditional pool hall. Three tables equally spaced apart were covered with traditional green cloth. The wood shone in the Tiffany-style billiard light hanging above each table. Three cue racks containing chalk, racks, and the essential cues hung on the walls, each assigned to their particular table. A colorful poster of the rules of billiard etiquette hung on the far wall.

EJ selected two cues from the rack on the wall and weighed each one in her hands. She handed the blue one to Dee.

"Now," she said seriously. "There are five keys to a good game of pool. She gathered the balls from the pockets and centered them in the ball rack.

"I'm all ears," Dee said, using the green cue chalk to coat the tip of her cue. When she looked up EJ was gazing at her from head to foot. She had made time for a pedicure; her toenails were painted a shade of bright red that made her feel sexy. Her skin was tanned from being out in the sun today, her hair down around her shoulders.

"No, you're all woman."

Dee felt herself blush at her comment and a little thrill criss-crossed down her spine.

"Here are my tips. Hold the cue properly, line up the shot, watch the cue ball rebound, and don't bet anything you can't afford to lose."

"You said there were five. What's the fifth?"

"Beer, an absolute must for a good game." EJ flagged down the waitress they'd seen earlier and ordered two of what she was drinking. While waiting for their drinks, EJ demonstrated rule number one. When she didn't quite get the proper hold, EJ stepped behind her and put her hand over hers. Their bodies weren't touching but they were pretty darn close. EJ smelled like cinnamon and Dee could feel the heat from her body. She thought she felt EJ's hands shaking.

The waitress arrived and, after a few quick swallows, EJ demonstrated the other rules. Dee was a quick study, pocketing quite a few balls in their first two games.

"How am I supposed to make this shot?" she asked midway through their third game. The cue ball was at an odd angle from the four ball, and she had tried unsuccessfully several times to line up the shot.

Dee knew that EJ was completely distracted watching her bend over her stick and line up her different shots. By the look on EJ's face the view of her butt was competing with the view down the front of her shirt for EJ's attention. EJ didn't have to let her win; she was losing because of the diversion.

"Like this," EJ said, stepping behind her when she leaned over the table, her stick outstretched in front of her. EJ molded the front of her body to her back. She stiffened in surprise then relaxed and felt EJ's nipples harden.

Suddenly it was very difficult to breathe and she arched her back into EJ. "What are your plans for the rest of the evening?"

EJ's warm breath on her neck, her husky voice in her ear made Dee shudder, and she didn't even try to hide her reaction. Dee felt her stiff nipples press against her back and the heat that started between her legs spread over her entire body.

She had played pool before, but never under the watchful eyes of someone like EJ. EJ followed her every move with smoldering eyes, and more than once Dee caught her looking down her shirt. She never thought a game of pool could be foreplay. She bent over the table, practically straddling the corner pocket, and having EJ watch her glide the long stick smoothly through her long fingers was a complete turn-on.

EJ pushed forward and Dee's mound pressed harder into the edge of the table. Her breath caught and she lost her grip on the stick, causing it to thump several times on the table. EJ started to move back and forth and Dee's clit hardened in response. She couldn't believe she was doing this. My God, she was practically fucking on a pool table and she didn't want to stop. EJ was pushing her pelvis into her ass and the exquisite pressure of impending orgasm began. A few more minutes of this and it would all be over but the afterglow. She was completely out of control and refused to stop.

"You two had better get a room."

EJ jerked back, the unrelenting pressure letting up instantly. Dee stifled a whimper.

"Sorry about that," EJ said from behind her, her voice unsteady. When Dee was finally able to turn around she saw EJ's hands were shaking, her face flushed from passion. EJ was as close to coming as she'd been.

"We're the ones that should be sorry. Sorry for interrupting, but this is a public place, you know," Rose said from behind EJ.

"No, that's all right, Rose. I should be apologizing. I'm afraid I...uh..."

Rose and Vivian laughed. "Yes, we know what you were...uh." Rose mimicked EJ's words.

Dee finally found her voice. "Could this get any more embarrassing?"

"In another minute or two it would have."

She leaned back against the edge of the pool table and dropped her head in her hands, completely and utterly mortified.

"Do you play?"

Adam's question pierced the fog of Dana's daydream. "Once or twice," Dana replied vaguely, not really answering him.

"Emery is a shark. Never, ever let her talk you into a game. You will lose everything."

The second floor was made up of four bedrooms, each decorated in a combination of modern and traditional style. Each room had a theme, the nautical one Dana's favorite. But Emery's bedroom completely took her breath away. She hung back as the others left.

The room was large, at least twenty feet square. The thick tan carpet made her want to take off her shoes and wiggle her toes. The walls were a shade of blue that mirrored the water in St. Martin. Abstract artwork dotted the walls, the bold shades bringing out the colors in the bed linen. The king-size bed dominated the room, the large pillows creating an open invitation to snuggle down and relax. The bed was flanked by two nightstands. On top of one a mid-size alarm clock rested in the center, while the other held a pad of paper and a pen next to a cordless phone in a small charger. There was no television in the room to distract its occupants from anything other than what this room was designed for—making love. This room screamed passion, desire, and sensuality.

Or did only she see that when she studied this room? Sure, everybody looked at someone's bed and thought about sex, wondered what they were like making love in that sacred place. Her hands started to tremble, her knees grew weak, and her breath came in spurts as she took in Emery's bed. She had experienced Emery's passion, desire, and sensuality and knew that she would never be the same again.

The image of the countless times she and Emery had made love danced around in her head. Unconsciously she stepped closer to the bed. Her heart beat faster and her body flushed, the soft pressure in her clit increasing to a rapid pounding.

She trailed her fingers over the thick bedspread. God, she wanted Emery again. She needed her touch, her soft caresses, her demanding kisses. She'd tried and failed to capture an orgasm as powerful as every one she had with Emery. There was no comparison, and her own hands left her so unfulfilled that lately she'd stopped trying. Had Emery ruined her for any other woman? "Jesus, Dana," she said aloud. She had to get out of here before she did something stupid like grab the pillow in search of Emery's scent.

Her heart stopped beating when she turned away from the bed. Emery was standing in the doorway and, judging by her expression, had been there for quite some time. Dana opened her mouth to speak but nothing came out. She had no idea what to say. She wanted to say, "Come in, close and lock the door, and take me in your arms. Kiss me, touch me, make me weak with desire. Make me come again and again and again. Take me."

But she didn't. She fought against her need and the mirror of desire written all over Emery's face. She couldn't. They had an agreement that now theirs was nothing more than a professional relationship. There was too much to lose for everyone involved, and she would not be the cause.

Getting a grip on her emotions, she walked toward Emery. Dark eyes blistering with desire never left her face, and Dana stopped directly in front of her. Inches separated them and she knew that if she gave any indication, Emery would fulfill her dreams. Time stood still. The world stopped rotating. The sounds of the party downstairs disappeared. No one existed except Emery standing in front of her, pinning her with that look that she knew so well. Emery wanted to eat her alive.

A thousand thoughts warred in her head. She fought dozens of battles in her body. Forces stronger than her will threatened to harness the power of their desire and take Emery and her to that place they both knew so well. The air around them beat with sexual tension. One touch. That's all it would take from either of them and they would completely forget the dozens of people downstairs. She wanted it, and the look in Emery's eyes was one she had seen countless times just before she was swept away in delicious pleasure.

This was so much harder than she'd thought it would be—this pretending not to feel anything for Emery, not to want her touch again, experience her passion, revel in her desire. She had completely underestimated the impact Emery would continue to have on her.

Finally, before she knew she wouldn't be able to do it, she sidestepped around Emery and prayed that her legs wouldn't collapse as she walked quickly down the hall.

Chapter Eighteen

D ana caught up with the others as the tour ended at the rear of the house. She paid little attention to those around her, concentrating instead on catching her breath and trying to calm her rattled nerves. It took several minutes before she felt relaxed enough to appreciate her surroundings.

This was not a patio, this was an oasis. Under her feet lay slabs of flagstone raggedly cut and laid to form a wonderfully smooth surface. The stone bordered the large crystal-clear blue pool on three sides, the fourth side almost disappearing into the mountainside behind the house. Dana realized it was a zero-edge pool and looked closer. She had seen one of these at a hotel she stayed at on a trip last year to Hawaii. The pool was designed to produce a visual effect of water extending to the horizon, and this was a spectacular one.

The lights around the pool were in fact gas-lit torches, giving the area a warm, soft glow. A sparkling array of lights bounced off the blue walls inside the still water. Comfortable-looking chairs and matching tables were strategically placed around the area, creating an intimate space for conversation without being rude. To her left was a cooking island complete with outdoor range and oven, a bar for casual seating, and a large cover over the entire area.

This was a place where Emery could come after the end of a long day with a glass of wine, put her feet in the water, and unwind. The soft sound of water cascading over the edge created a tranquil spot in an otherwise frenzied world.

Emery couldn't wait any longer. She had watched Dana throughout the evening, and when Dana had gone upstairs with Adam and the others, she'd had to follow. She often dreamed of taking Dana upstairs, their fingers intertwined, their destination known.

When she saw Dana in her bedroom, her heart couldn't decide whether to dance or stop. Dana was standing beside her bed with a look of longing that set her already smoldering body on fire. She watched her for several moments, not saying anything, afraid to even breathe lest she break the spell. It felt like hours that she stood in the doorway, drinking in the woman who had captured her imagination, her interest, her respect, and her common sense.

When Dana walked toward her she thought she was going to kiss her. She hoped and prayed she would kiss her. Her body begged Dana to kiss her. But she didn't. She saw the conflicting emotions in Dana's eyes, saw the strong will take over as she stepped around her and walked away.

"Enjoying yourself?" Dana jumped, obviously surprised, their bodies touching lightly. Emery's body reacted immediately.

"I didn't hear you," Dana replied, stepping away from her.

"Sorry, I didn't mean to scare you." However the feel of Dana's body against hers, if only for an instant, felt fabulous.

"I guess I didn't hear you come up. You have a beautiful home. Your view is stunning." Dana lifted her hand to indicate the landscape in front of them.

She walked toward Dana and stood beside her. They were shoulder to shoulder, gazing at the lights of the city out beyond her property. "Thank you. When I was hunting a place to build I told the realtor I could create a house, but I couldn't create what only Mother Nature could." This was her retreat, her sanctuary, her refuge from the pressures of her life.

"Give me her name, she did an excellent job."

She risked a glance at Dana's face. The lights from the torches cast a soft glow on her high cheekbones, the light from the pool reflecting in her eyes. Dana was more beautiful tonight than any other time they'd been together. She wanted to hold Dana again, caress her face, taste her, feel her body pressed against hers, her passion rise and crest in her arms.

They stood like that for several minutes before Dana spoke. "Yes."

Emery's static heart skipped again. *What? Yes to what?* Yes to what she was thinking? Yes to what she was imagining? Yes to what she was dreaming, what she craved every night?

"To your question. Am I enjoying myself?" Dana's soft smile sent her stomach rolling in circles. "Yes, I am, very much."

"I'm glad." For a few minutes they said nothing. The silence between them made her nervous. She didn't trust herself not to turn and kiss Dana.

"The invitation was plus one." Emery ventured into the place she wasn't sure she wanted to be.

"Yes, I know," Dana replied simply.

"You could have brought someone. A date," she said. Dana turned slightly to look at her. It was just dark enough she couldn't see what was in her eyes.

"I know."

"It wouldn't have been a problem, you know." She was babbling. Dana stepped just a fraction closer, and this time Emery could see what was in her eyes.

"I know I could have brought a guest. I know it could have been a woman, and I know it wouldn't have been a problem. But this is a business function as much as it is a social event. I do not call attention to whom I'm seeing, if anyone, at these kinds of things. It can be awkward and I have enough trouble being taken seriously in this male-dominated industry. I don't need the distraction of filthy minds imagining me and my lover together."

The irritation in Dana's voice and the anger in her eyes stunned her. Where had that come from? All she'd wanted to do was let Dana know that it was okay for her to bring her significant other, if she had one.

"Dana." Emery began before she knew what she was going to say. What *was* she going to say? Was she going to tell Dana how much she missed her, how much she missed hearing her laugh, her quick wit, her dazzling smile? Was she going to ask her to stay? She couldn't even think straight anymore.

Dana turned away from her. They were the only ones on the patio. "You'd better get back to your other guests. We don't want anybody to think I'm monopolizing your time. They might get the wrong idea." Dana kept her gaze locked on the horizon to their left.

Her message was very clear, and as much as Emery wanted to stay and argue the point, she knew Dana was right. God, Dana was so much stronger than she was. "You're right. I was just making the rounds. Enjoy the rest of the evening," she managed to get out without letting her hurt and disappointment show.

The cold was starting to penetrate Dana's thin dress and she started to turn to leave. A voice behind her stopped her.

"I'm glad you came tonight, Dana."

Oh, for God's sake, she didn't need this right now. Plastering on her most benign expression she politely turned around. "Hello, Sharon." She noted the full glass of red wine in her hand.

"Emery knows how to throw a party. You know, I think she lives a charmed life."

She didn't want to hear how charmed, but there was no way to politely get out of this conversation. At least not at this moment. However, she refused to give Sharon any encouragement to continue.

"She has this great house," Sharon said, waving her arm, the contents of her glass sloshing over the side. "Doesn't this pool just make you want to take off your clothes and swim naked under the stars?" Dana was hoping this wouldn't be a repeat of when Sharon practically drank her lunch, but it appeared she was headed in that direction without any regard of the impression she was leaving with Dana.

"Did your husband come with you tonight, Sharon? I don't think I've met him," she said, trying to steer the conversation into a safer direction.

Sharon practically gulped the remaining wine in her glass. "My husband hasn't *come* with me in years, if you know what I mean." Sharon slurred her words.

OMG! This *was not* a conversation Dana wanted to have with anyone at this party, and certainly not with Sharon. Her stomach turned just trying not to think about *that* visual.

"How about I call you a cab, Sharon?" Under normal circumstances Dana would have taken her arm and led her to the front door. But she didn't want to touch Sharon for fear she would take it the wrong way.

"I'm not ready to leave. I want to talk with you some more. I enjoyed our conversation at lunch. I thought we could continue it. How about over there, where it's nice and quiet." Sharon pointed to a set of chairs on the other side of the pool.

"I'm afraid I can't. I was just getting ready to go." She saw the spark of opportunity flash across Sharon's face and quickly added, "I've got another party to go to this evening, and I'm running late already." She started walking toward the doors that led back into the house.

She said her good-byes, making sure Emery was with a group of people when she did. Exhaling deeply she waited on the front porch for the valet to bring around her car. She'd never experienced a night like this before. As she slid behind the wheel, she hoped she never would again.

Chapter Nineteen

The flight to Hong Kong was long and nerve-racking. It was the third week in January, and by the time Emery got off the plane she was about to crawl out of her skin. Adam had sat her and Dana next to each other, and even though business class wasn't nearly as cramped as coach, it was still way too close for Emery's frayed senses.

Since their words at her party they had maintained a strictly professional relationship. Actually, truth be told, she had made herself scarce most of the time, not wanting to see Dana unless others were present. No one seemed to notice the chill in the air between them, but Dana avoided her eyes as well.

After finally clearing customs she slid into the back of the taxi. Her luggage had been selected for random inspection, and she had told Dana to go ahead to the hotel. Their driver had been waiting patiently at the exit from baggage claim with a sign that simply had MARTIN written in thick black marker. She had given Dana that car, and when her bags cleared, she grabbed the next taxi in line.

She was tired, having not slept any on the twenty-hour flight and not much for the week leading up to this trip. In addition to preparing for the meetings she would have with the executives and employees of the company they were acquiring, she'd dreamed of Dana. Dana riding a bike, the wind in her hair. Dana strolling through a local marketplace in St. Martin, her shorts exposing far too much leg for Emery's itching hands to resist.

❖

The offices of Stephenson Electronics were located in an industrial park about an hour from their hotel. Dana sat quietly as Emery read the papers in a manila folder she pulled from her briefcase as the driver smoothly maneuvered through the busy morning traffic.

She took the opportunity to study Emery out of the corner of her eye. Emery was wearing a dark-blue Anne Klein suit with a blue-and-white-striped collared blouse. She was professional without being overtly powerful, yet Dana knew there would be no doubt as to who was in charge today.

Dana followed the thin pinstripes down Emery's jacket sleeve and settled on her hands. Her fingers were long and her nails short, a clear coat of polish shiny in the morning sun. She didn't recognize the ring that Emery wore on the third finger of her right hand and wondered if it was a Christmas gift from an admirer. Emery's hands were steady as she held the folder, but Dana remembered the times when they trembled with desire.

She swallowed hard and forced her eyes off the hands that knew her so intimately, had caressed every inch of her body, had gone inside her, stroked, teased, and pleasured her and brought her to orgasm dozens of times. She intended to look out the window but, as if they had a mind of their own, her eyes went directly to Emery's face and directly to her eyes.

Her breath hitched because she knew Emery had caught her looking—or was it longing? Desire burned in Emery's eyes and her stomach flipped when Emery licked her lips. Ever so slowly, Emery leaned toward her.

She wanted Emery to kiss her. Wanted to feel her warm lips on her face, her soft tongue in her mouth. Instantly her clit throbbed in equal time with her racing pulse.

Emery wanted her too. Dana could see it in her eyes, read it in her body language. She'd seen that message often enough to know what would happen next. And she was powerless to stop it. But suddenly the driver slammed on his brakes and cursed.

"Shit," Emery said, shaking her head after the car came to a stop.

"Sorry, ladies," the driver said in a thick accent. "Just another mile or so," he added, accelerating around the car in front of him.

Emery jumped at the opportunity to gather the contents of the file that had skittered across her lap and settled around her feet. What was she about to do? She was seconds away from kissing Dana. She had no idea what had happened other than feeling like she'd been caught in a vortex pulling her toward Dana's lips.

She had to get control of herself or this situation would be a disaster waiting to happen. She was stronger than this, her mind stronger than her body. It always had been and she needed to ensure it stayed that way. She would not do anything to jeopardize everything she had worked for and didn't intend to potentially ruin Dana in the ensuing tsunami.

Her hands shook and she hoped the movement of the car masked her turmoil. When she had caught Dana staring at her hands she'd known what she was thinking. Her own hands had tingled with the memory of touching Dana.

The tension in the rear of the Town Car was thick and Emery believed it was her role to diffuse it. But she had no idea how. She was afraid if she opened her mouth she'd tell the driver to turn around and take them back to the hotel. So she said nothing.

❖

One, two, three, breathe. One, two, three, breathe. Dana counted her rhythmic cadence lap after lap in the cool water. The day had been excruciating and she needed to burn off her pent-up energy; swimming was the perfect release. After the near-kiss this morning, she couldn't look at Emery the rest of the day without her pulse jumping, her heart skipping, and a flash of heat scorching a trail through her body. She had never been as completely aroused and on edge as she had been all day.

She had watched Emery alternatively in awe and in lust as she managed the Stephenson employees. She acknowledged their anger, smoothly deflected their hostility, and never lost control of the room. Meeting after meeting she gave each group her full attention, and Dana had been enthralled at how well she managed it all.

But when their eyes met, the outside world disappeared and she felt the intensity of Emery's gaze. At the dinner with the Stephenson board of directors, Emery really shone. Dana had never seen anyone so poised, sophisticated, and completely in control. She answered every question without hesitation, rattled off facts and figures like they were in front of her. Not only did Dana's body react to Emery's nearness, but her mind did as well. She had read somewhere that the way to a woman's heart was through her head. Emery was the complete package and she wanted to rip it open.

One, two, three, breathe. One, two, three, breathe. Stroke after stroke Dana pulled herself through the clear water until she was almost too exhausted to get out.

Emery paced inside the luxurious room. After the long flight and the endless meetings today with the Stephenson employees she should be exhausted, but she was restless. She turned on her iPad and selected a book from her library, but ended up reading the same page twice. She flipped through the channels on the large television more than a dozen times, but nothing held her interest for more than a few minutes. She even pulled a stack of information and reports on Stephenson from her briefcase, and for the first time she could remember, even work didn't hold her attention.

The mini-bar had a wide selection of liquor, and she poured herself a hefty serving of Crown Royal with just a splash of Coke. She hoped the alcohol would relax her enough to sleep but doubted it. Adam had again reserved adjoining rooms so tonight would be another sleepless night imagining Dana naked in the bed next door.

Emery pushed the button on the wall, the curtains soundlessly sliding open to reveal the Hong Kong skyline. Dozens of buildings filled the dark sky, a smattering of lights creating a crosshatch on the various floors. How many of those lights were used by people still working?

Normally she would be one of those people who were on first-name basis with the night cleaning crew to get ahead or sometimes just to keep up. She rarely thought twice about it. Work was her life, her ambition to be the best in everything she did. Her entire career had been focused on moving up. With all the demands on her, her personal life was as full as she wanted it to be.

But lately she felt like something was missing. She couldn't put her finger on it, but it was like looking for something she couldn't describe, taste, or touch. One of those I'll-know-it-when-I-see-it kind of things. That kind of ambiguity made her nuts, unsettled her and made her search that much harder. She was a facts-and-figures thinker, and this kind of abstract situation felt like it was just out of reach.

Maybe the cruise had thrown her off kilter. Her illness certainly had. She had never been away from work for more than a week at a time, and her three-week forced sabbatical was stressful, to say the least. But she'd been back at work for six months, and surely by now she would be back into the familiar routine. But as each day went by she felt more and more out of sorts.

She opened the heavy sliding-glass door and stepped onto the balcony. A warm breeze ruffled her hair, the air thick with humidity. She was just about to return to the coolness of her room when motion below her caught her eye.

A woman was walking toward the pool on the roof of the conference center attached to their hotel. From her vantage point two floors higher, Emery could make out the No Diving and FOUR FEET SIX INCHES lettering spaced evenly around the perimeter of the rectangular pool. The woman was bundled in the same white terry-cloth robe that hung in her own closet on the other side of the room. She placed a towel and a small bag on one of the chairs and untied the robe. She looked vaguely familiar, and Emery stepped closer to the railing to get a better look.

Her heart stopped when the woman slid the robe off her shoulders and laid it over the back of the chair. It was Dana, and she watched, mesmerized as Dana pulled her hair up into a ponytail and began a series of exercises designed to warm up her muscles. She lifted her arms over her head, clasped her hands together, and stretched first to the left, then the right, bending at the waist and finally stretching backward. The ice in Emery's cocktail clinked against the side of her glass as her hands shook.

Dana wore an electric-blue, one-piece suit cut high on the hips and low in the back, complementing her trim figure and full breasts. Moving her arms in a butterfly motion, she walked across the tile patio and stepped into the pool. At the bottom step she didn't hesitate, but slid into the water and started swimming across the long pool.

Emery had no idea how long she stood there watching Dana, but she was spellbound as she completed each lap. Back and forth she swam, her long arms cutting through the water like she was born to it. She was practiced and graceful, the water churning at her feet the only ripple in the pool. Emery caught glimpses of her back and butt as Dana executed what looked like perfect flip turns at the end of each lap.

Thirty-five minutes later Dana finally stopped and climbed out of the pool. Water dripped off her long, sleek body and trailed a path behind her as she walked back across the deck. Her muscles gleamed in the night-lights, her hair was plastered down her back. Dana must have swum regularly to have kept up that pace almost effortlessly.

Dana lay down on the lounge chair, her legs out in front of her. Emery could see her breasts heaving up and down from the exertion, and she unconsciously did the same. Her mind flashed back to other times and events where their breathing matched a similar frenetic pace, and the tightening in her groin kicked up a notch.

Dana finally stood, and when she turned around and bent over to pick something up off the ground, giving Emery a perfect look at her backside, Emery dropped her glass. The breaking of the glass on the cement balcony was loud and shattered the spell she was under. "Shit," she exclaimed, at the mixture of glass, ice, and brown liquid scattered at her feet. She glanced back to Dana, who had looked up at the noise.

Their eyes locked and she felt the power of Dana's magnetism. Her body came alive simply from Dana's gaze. She was too far away to read what was in Dana's eyes, and she was glad Dana couldn't see hers either. It was getting harder to maintain a professional distance when every time she looked at Dana her heart flipped and memories of their time together flashed in her brain like a kaleidoscope and through her body like a hot iron.

Only once did she see a similar thought cross Dana's face. That was during their first meeting after the cruise, and she had immediately shut it down. Dana seemed to be much better at controlling her emotions than Emery. Or at least it looked that way. She felt herself blush at being caught watching and was grateful she was too far away for Dana to see her. Dana finally broke eye contact, gathered her things, and, after covering her body with the robe, walked back across the pool deck toward the doors.

Emery cleaned up the broken glass and made herself another drink, this one stronger than the last. She downed it quickly when she heard the muffled sounds next door, indicating Dana had returned to her room.

Emery was a mess. She was fighting the voice in her head that told her to open the connecting door and the other voice that told her to stay away. Her body was on fire. She wanted to touch Dana, smell her unique scent, hold her as she trembled with desire in her arms. Dana was a passionate, engaged lover, demanding that Emery satisfy her.

Against her will she walked to the door, unlocked it, and opened her side. She put her ear to the door and heard rustling sounds on the other side. She couldn't make out exactly what they were, but the sound of running water in the background was unmistakable.

She felt like a fool. Here she was, a successful, rich, and powerful businesswoman, and she had her ear to the door like a kid trying to hear what her parents are saying in the next room. She moved her hand across the door as if caressing Dana's body. God, she was pitiful.

The water stopped and she waited a few minutes. Her heart was pounding, her clit throbbing, and the voices in her head warring against each other loudly. She felt weak and slightly dizzy as the sensations blasted through her body. She turned slightly, her forehead pressed against Dana's door. All it would take was one knock. One discreet rapping of her shaking hand on the door and she could release the tension that had been growing in her body for months.

She and Dana could be together again. Who would know? No one. It wasn't like there was a card reader on this door that recorded who went through it and when. Even if it had, what was to say they weren't simply having a discussion about the meetings today or planning their strategy for tomorrow? What a bunch of crap. She wanted Dana and she wanted her bad.

She hesitated. She needed to be strong, to resist the urge that her body was demanding be satisfied. She could do this, she said to herself, in direct contrast to the fact that her knuckles on her right hand were resting on the door just waiting to rap. She remembered another time she'd tried to resist this pull.

EJ knocked on the door, harder this time. It sounded louder than it probably was in the quiet hall. It was one fifteen in the morning, and it had been over an hour since she'd seen anyone. Unable to sleep, she'd taken a walk around the main deck. Actually, she'd made several trips, hardly paying any attention to the deck chairs lined up in neat rows or the towels stacked high with razor precision on the shelves. The night was warm and, unlike EJ's insides, the wind relatively calm.

She and Dee had agreed that tonight they would sleep in their respective cabins. Lord knew they both needed a good night's sleep after several days of snorkeling, scuba diving, and long walks on beachfronts. During their nights, and sometimes in remote places during the day, they explored each other to the point of exhaustion. After the movie she had walked Dee to her cabin and, after a semi-chaste kiss on the lips, returned to her own.

So why was she here, standing outside Dee's door? She was agitated, her nerves almost raw, and her mind was jetting around in a thousand places. She wanted Dee. She wasn't just horny. She desired Dee, yearned for her touch, craved the taste of her. Not just her body, but everything about Dee turned her on. She was confident in her sexuality, which EJ found overwhelming. There was something exciting about a woman who took off her own clothes because she wanted you to touch her, knew she was going to give her body to another person, wanted to be touched.

When Dee took control of her own needs EJ was completely lost. She couldn't describe how it made her feel when Dee met her halfway for a kiss or pulled her to her or took her hand and put it exactly where she wanted it. She had never felt this way with a woman. She always found women sexy, but never in a basic way like this that made her absolutely crazy.

Her legs were shaking and the seconds dragged by. She debated with herself if she should knock again or go back to her own cabin. She knew she wouldn't sleep without Dee beside her. Berating herself for being so out of control she turned to walk back down the hall, then heard the door open.

"EJ?" Dee asked, confusion in her voice.

She turned around and felt like a complete fool. She was acting like a teenager who couldn't control her impulses. She was a grown woman, for crying out loud. An important businesswoman with the responsibility of thousands of employees and millions of dollars, and she couldn't even keep her pants on. At that moment she almost hated herself.

"Couldn't sleep?" Dee asked softly. She was leaning on the doorjamb, her robe tied loosely at the waist.

"No." She shifted her weight from foot to foot, burying her hands in the pockets of her pants to keep from reaching out and touching Dee. She refused to pressure Dee to change her mind about spending the night apart.

"Me either."

Dee slammed the door and pressed her against it. Dee's hands dispensed with her belt in two seconds, and Dee was working on her zipper when she grasped her wrists, stopping her.

"Hey, slow down. We have all night."

Dee's breathing was quick, her heart beating hard. "I don't care. I want you now, I need you like this. Let me, please."

She kept hold of Dee's hands and gently kissed her. Dee tried to deepen the kiss but she pulled away and looked deeply into Dee's eyes.

"I can't say no to you," EJ admitted.

Emery shuddered at the memory, her legs shaking badly as she stared at the nondescript door in front of her. They both had too much to lose. She had worked too hard to throw it all away for one night. And it wouldn't be enough. One night in Dana's arms would be only the beginning of her wanting, no, needing even more. She couldn't do it, wouldn't do it.

She closed the door silently so that Dana would not be aware of just how close she had come to giving in to her desire.

Emery stood back and took a deep breath. Much, much more than a door separated them now.

Chapter Twenty

Emery watched Dana sleep. She was almost more beautiful when she slept. Her face was relaxed and her eyes twitched ever so slightly. On the cruise Emery had watched her sleep, the deep sleep of sexual exhaustion. Even then she was radiant, the telltale signs of good sex flushing her skin and giving her a sensuous glow.

The week had been exhausting. She and Dana had traveled to over a dozen Stephenson facilities around the region, and by the time they were on the plane headed back to the US they had met with over six thousand employees, had twenty-four meetings and countless dinners. Dana was exhausted and Emery was hoarse.

She detected the fine lines of exhaustion and tension around Dana's eyes and felt guilty for having put them there. She never wanted to do anything that would put a mark on Dana's flawless skin, but this week had.

She couldn't deny the consuming attraction she felt for Dana. She had stopped trying and had shifted tactics to simply manage it. Simply—what a joke that word was. There was nothing simple about it.

During the entire week she'd known exactly where Dana was. She'd sought her out when she was onstage speaking to the employees crowded in the auditorium, known if she was in the large room, and felt her presence down the hall in the hotel.

She had no idea how Dana felt about her. She felt like she was as transparent as a window, but could never quite get a read on what Dana was thinking. Dana was certainly upholding her end of their agreement. Was their relationship over for her? Had she been able to move it to the file that held her cruise pictures and other souvenirs?

Emery sure as shit hadn't.

❖

"Dana, how are you?"

Angst gripped Dana when she heard Sharon's voice coming from the doorway to her office. She had spent all week trying to catch up on the work that had piled up while she and Emery were in Hong Kong. She braced herself, smiled, and looked up. She kept her pen in her hand, hoping Sharon would see she was working and not stay long.

"I'm fine, Sharon. Good to see you again. Is the board meeting over?" It was the first Monday of the quarter, the regularly scheduled day for board meetings.

"Yes, I was just headed out for some dinner. Would you like to join me?"

Shit. Dana had no desire to have dinner with Sharon but knew she had to. In the corporate world when a board member, in this case also known as the boss's boss, invites you to dinner, you go. As simple as that. It was political suicide not to, even if you had previous plans.

"I'm sorry, Sharon, I'd love to, but I can't get away tonight."

Sharon's face showed her surprise at Dana's refusal. Sharon studied her for a few moments before she stepped into her office and closed the door behind her.

Fuck.

"Are you trying to avoid me, Dana?"

"Of course not," she replied quickly. "I just wasn't expecting you, or anyone else for that matter, this late and I—"

"Can't get away tonight."

"Yes, I am sorry," she said carefully. She saw the disapproval on Sharon's face. "I can put it on my calendar for next quarter," she said, hoping Sharon would accept the alternative. She reached for her BlackBerry.

"Have you given any more thought to our conversation?"

Sharon didn't have to provide any details as to which conversation she was referring. It was never far from Dana's mind.

"Sharon," she said, sitting straighter in her chair. She still held her favorite pen, a kind of security blanket. "With all due respect, this conversation makes me uncomfortable. Emery is my boss, and not only that but I respect her tremendously. What she has done to turn Martin around in such a short period of time is amazing. The employees have a very high opinion of her and are putting forth the extra effort we need. The issues that Martin had in the past are virtually nonexistent because of her and her leadership team."

"I know all that, Dana." Sharon waved her hand as if dismissing her comment. "But I don't trust her."

She was determined not to fidget or break eye contact first. She believed everything she'd just said about Emery and wanted nothing to do with Sharon's behind-the-back spying. "Sharon, shouldn't you be having this conversation with Marcus? He's the chairman of the board. If you've lost faith in one of the members of the leadership team, he's the one you need to talk to."

"He's in bed with Emery."

"I beg your pardon?"

"Not that way," Sharon said dismissively. "And that's something else that concerns me, but we'll get to it in a minute."

Her antennae rose a little higher at that statement.

"He thinks the sun rises and sets in Emery. He is anything but objective."

"What about one of the other board members?" She could not believe she was counseling Sharon.

"They're all the same. I told you it was still an old-boys club and that we girls need to stick together. Now as for the other thing." Sharon leaned forward in her chair and looked over her shoulder as if to check that no one was listening. "Did you know Emery is a homosexual?"

She bit back a laugh. Sharon was so serious it was comical, but this was not the time to correct her choice of labels or add her name to the list. "What Emery does in her personal time is none of my business." *And as long as it doesn't affect the company it shouldn't be any of yours either.*

"But doesn't that bother you? I mean you have to travel with her, spend a lot of time with her."

"Emery is always a complete professional with everyone around her. She would never do anything that would jeopardize the reputation of Martin Engineering, and that includes any inappropriate behavior."

"I just don't like it. It's not natural." Sharon pursed her lips together tightly.

"Why did the board hire Emery?" Sharon looked at her, obviously confused at the change of topic. "You hired her because she was the most qualified to turn this company around and restore shareholder confidence. And she's done that. Exactly what you hired her to do. If she's not doing that, then as a member of Martin's board you have an obligation and fiduciary responsibility to the shareholders to take action. Now, if you'll excuse me." She stood and walked around from behind her desk and toward her door. "I really do have to finish a few things tonight." She opened the door, effectively ending the conversation.

❖

Emery was amazing. Just watching her made Dana's heart pound a little faster and her breathing shallow. And she was able to simply look at her without being afraid of getting caught ogling her boss. She, Emery, and a few of the Martin Engineering senior staff were attending a conference of engine manufacturers in the convention center the first week in March. Emery was one of the speakers, and the room had filled beyond capacity at least fifteen minutes before she was even scheduled to appear.

As she watched Emery speak, she was amazed at Emery's calm, engaging manner onstage in front of hundreds of people. She had them laughing at the right places, on the edge of their seats in others, and spent over forty-five minutes after the session answering questions. No wonder she was a fabulous and successful CEO, a change agent, a leader. She had charisma, energy, and a way of connecting with everyone she spoke to.

Since coming to work at Martin, she had had many opportunities to see Emery in action. She never lost her temper, never raised her voice, and never swore. She was professional without being cold and, from the hallway chatter Dana overheard, had the respect of the employees at Martin.

She sat back in the chair and couldn't help comparing the woman on the stage with the woman she'd met on the *Seafair*. EJ had a great sense of humor, laughed a lot, and approached each day with a carefree manner and absolutely no plans. EJ was charming, entertaining, and fascinating. She practically oozed sensuality and had an air of confidence and mystery that was captivating. Her telltale signs of stress had visibly lessened every day. No wonder she was ordered to rest. Keeping herself in check had to be absolutely exhausting.

Emery was more subdued, her movements clearly thought out and at times almost scripted. She was charismatic and people were naturally drawn to her. She was professional, brilliant with numbers, and undeniably in charge. The signs of stress grew more pronounced every day.

After the speakers were done for the day and before the social hour, Dana managed to escape for a few minutes of peace and quiet to go next door to the King Tut exhibit. Slowly she strolled through the maze of rooms, each holding a myriad of artifacts that had been discovered with the boy king.

As she read the information card under a chipped chalice, she felt eyes watching her. She had had this same feeling for the past few minutes and turned around to see a woman looking at her. She smiled politely and headed for the next area of the exhibit.

The woman followed her from room to room, and Dana saw that she wasn't paying any attention to the items on display but appeared to be totally focused on her.

"I'm sorry, do I know you?" She was fed up with the woman who had not so subtly followed her throughout the exhibit hall. The woman kept staring at her and she felt like she was under surveillance. More surprising, she didn't even try to evade Dana as she walked across the room and stopped in front of her.

"We were on the same cruise several months ago," the woman replied, her eyes running up and down the length of Dana's body. She was sitting on a bench, her legs crossed.

Dana was shocked at the double hit the woman casually tossed her way. First was the blatant cruising. She had been the object of such appraising looks before, but none felt as slimy as the one that just came from this woman. Second, and more important, was her reference to the cruise. Had she seen her and Emery together? If she had, what was she going to do with that piece of information? Did she have any idea who she or Emery was? Was this going to be a problem?

All of these thoughts shot through her head in the second it took her to put a confused expression on her face. "I'm sorry?" Dana said, deciding not to immediately confirm that she was, in fact, on the cruise. She needed to see just how much this woman knew.

"The cruise…to the southern Caribbean. Two thousand lesbians in bikinis. Ring a bell?"

Thanks to years of training Dana remained outwardly calm. Inside, however, her heart was racing and her throat very dry. Out of the corner of her eye she saw that no one was near enough to overhear their conversation. Thank God for that small favor.

She took a harder look at the woman. She looked older by about ten years, and sun and alcohol had not been kind to her. She was rail thin, her hair way too black to be natural, and her voice raspy from too many cartons of cigarettes.

Her sixth sense told her to be careful. Other than the obvious, something about this woman set her antennae chirping.

"I'm sorry, have we met?" she asked, still not confirming that she was on the cruise. The woman looked vaguely familiar. "I'm terrible with names, and people look different in different settings."

The woman took a sip of her cocktail, her red lipstick leaving a clear imprint on the rim of the thick glass. She leaned in and Dana smelled the liquor on her breath. It was from more than the glass she held in her blue-veined hand. "Let me jog your memory. You were with that hot butch brunette. Tall, thin, and more than a little yummy."

She still wasn't sure where this conversation was going. She prayed that Emery wasn't close by or she knew exactly where it would go. Her heart felt like it had stopped. She knew immediately what the woman was going to do, and she braced herself.

"What can I do for you Ms…"

"Hastings. Camille Hastings."

The woman held out her hand in greeting. Dana didn't want to shake it, but she couldn't afford to piss this woman off, especially here.

"What can I do for you Ms. Hastings?" she repeated.

"Sit down, Dana," she said, patting the seat next to her. "Make yourself comfortable."

She didn't move. No way would she give this woman anything she asked for, and that included sitting beside her. She liked the psychological advantage of towering over her. The expression on her face clearly said she was waiting for an answer this time.

"Fuck me like I know you fucked her."

"Excuse me?" She couldn't even try to hide her shock.

"You heard me. I didn't stutter." She slurred the last word so it sounded more like *studder*.

She looked around and wished Camille was standing so they could move to a more private place to talk. However, Camille was staying put.

"I don't mean to be rude, Ms. Hastings, but I don't know what you're talking about. Now if you'll excuse me." Dana started to walk away on shaky legs.

"You two make a striking couple. What did they call it, the Power Suite?"

Dana stopped and turned around. The woman held out a magazine and she instinctively reached out and looked at the cover. It was an industry trade magazine, and Emery's success at turning around Martin was the feature article. Since Emery had referenced Dana often during the interview, the writer had insisted the photographer take several shots of the two of them together. She was looking at one of those photos now.

"Small world, isn't it?"

Her head spun and she was having a hard time comprehending what was actually happening. Finally she handed the magazine back to the woman. "What do you want?"

"I told you what I want. I don't think I can say it any plainer, but I can try."

She interrupted the woman before she could begin. "This really isn't the time to be having this conversation." She didn't want to have it at all, but especially not at an event where any one of the dozens of people could walk in at any time. Camille laughed and an icy chill ran down Dana's spine.

"You didn't waste any time getting down with Emery Barrett on the ship, so why waste time now?"

Holy Christ, she knows who Emery is. This was her worst nightmare and she knew she wouldn't wake up. She fought to remain calm. She couldn't let Camille see that she actually had her by the throat. "I don't think this is the place to talk about this." *I have to get this woman out of here before she makes a scene.*

"Don't run off, Dana," Camille said, her hand cold and clammy when she touched her forearm. "Emery is the last person who can help you with this."

She glanced around the room. Several people had entered and were making their way toward them.

Dana lowered her voice, hoping to encourage the Hastings woman to do the same. "And why is that?"

"Because I'll go to the Feds and she'll lose her job." When Dana snapped her head around in Camille's direction she continued. "I know about the government stipulations Martin is under. If any one in top management engages in fraud, deceit, or any other inappropriate, illegal, or immoral activity, Martin will lose their license to do business with the Feds. That, in effect, is a death sentence to your company."

When she didn't respond Camille kept talking. "One phone call to the hotline," she hesitated slightly, "or to your biggest competitor, and the rest is history. Not to mention your reputation."

"Why are you doing this?" Dana finally asked.

"Because I want you."

The undisguised leer in Camille's eyes turned her stomach. She had been the recipient of many unwanted advances, but none, including those of James Bethel, were as disgusting as what this woman was proposing. Obviously Camille was not above using her body to blackmail her into getting what she wanted.

"And you couldn't have just asked me out?" Even her own words sounded crazy, but she had to say something.

"Don't make me laugh. I watched you two on the ship. You were hot. You could barely keep your hands off each other. I saw you two on one of the decks. I must say you are quite beautiful when you come."

Camille dropped a picture on top of the magazine, and she felt as if the wind had been knocked out of her.

She remembered the scene as if it were yesterday. It was taken when she and Emery thought they were in an area where they couldn't be seen. Emery had her pinned to the wall, her hand down the front of her pants. Dana's hands were on Emery's breasts under her shirt and she was pinching her nipples. Emery's face was clearly visible in the reflection in the window behind Dana's head. The picture was obviously from a cell phone taken the instant Emery's fingers had entered her, causing her to come hard and fast.

Camille stood. "You have three days to decide. I'll call you at your office, and don't even think of not accepting my call." Camille brushed by her but thankfully not close enough for them to touch. "I just love digital cameras, don't you?"

Chapter Twenty-one

Stunned was nowhere near strong enough a word to describe how Dana felt. Staggered, shocked, horrified, sickened—the list could go on.

Could her life get any more bizarre? First it was three weeks of incredible sex and connection with Emery, who turned out to be her new boss, then Sharon's obvious attempt to get her to be her corporate spy, and now Camille Hastings. When did everything start to fall off the tracks?

"Excuse me, ma'am, are you all right?"

The voice to her left was tentative and pulled her out of her fog. She looked into the concerned face of one of the waiters that were floating around the room.

"You look a little pale. Can I get you anything?"

"No, I'm fine, thanks," she lied, loosening her shoulders to pull herself together. "Really, I'm fine," she added for emphasis.

The waiter left the room with a final look over his shoulder. Dana smiled and gave him an easy wave and followed right behind him.

She saw Camille Hastings putting on her coat and being escorted out the door by a short, overweight, silver-haired man. She breathed a sigh of relief knowing she wouldn't have to face her later tonight.

It took over ten minutes for her to weave her way through the crowd before she finally located Emery. Half a dozen twenty-something women surrounded her, and they appeared to be hanging on her every word. A pang of jealousy struck Dana in the stomach as she waited for a break in the conversation to announce she was leaving.

"Is everything all right?" Emery asked, a frown creasing her forehead.

"Yes, just a little headache that if I ignore will become a raging one. I'll see you tomorrow." More calmly than she felt, she walked toward the exit, feeling Emery's eyes watching her every step.

Back in her car Dana couldn't wait until she got home to find as much information as she could about Camille Hastings. Knowledge was power, and Dana was in no way going to let this woman blackmail or intimidate her. She pulled out her smartphone and in the darkness Googled Camille Hastings. The light from the screen was bright and she blinked several times, allowing her eyes to adjust to the glow. She scrolled through hits on several Camille Hastings, including Facebook and LinkedIn accounts, Web pages, and several academic and speaker notes. Nothing matched the woman she had met earlier, and Dana had just about given up when she clicked on one particularly interesting link.

"Holy fuck," she whispered inside her empty car. Warning bells chimed in her head, dread exploded in her gut, her breathing shallow and short. No wonder she looked familiar. Camille Hastings was James Bethel's twin sister.

Chapter Twenty-two

Dana sat in her car, dazed. What was she going to do? She was between shit and a shit hole, as her father would say, and how had she gotten here? One minute she was on a cruise, fully intending to while away the days exploring the southern Caribbean. Instead she met a beguiling, charming woman named EJ and explored her.

She remembered the night in Camille's photo. She and EJ had finished dinner late and were walking around the deck enjoying the cool breeze. Due to the late hour they were one of the few couples on deck, and they held hands as they dodged deck chairs, their voices soft in the night air.

She'd let out a shriek as EJ pulled her into an area adjacent to a locker that held towels for the pool, and that was where Camille had taken their picture.

Embarrassed over getting caught in a very compromising position, rage over Camille's threats, and fear that the woman would actually follow through on them battled for space in her brain. She had to tell Emery, warn her of Camille and what she might do, what she could do. Would Emery want her to have sex with Camille? Surely not, but then again she knew just how hard Emery had worked to get where she was. Was there nothing she wouldn't do to save herself, her reputation?

Dana pulled into her driveway hours later. She was mentally and physically exhausted as she stripped, took two sleeping pills, and crawled naked into bed.

❖

"Dana?" Emery's staff meeting was over and everyone was filing out of the large conference room adjacent to her office. Dana had not yet moved or even begun to gather her papers together. "Are you okay?" Without thinking she laid her hand on Dana's forearm. The contact seemed to pull Dana back from wherever she was.

Dana blinked a few times as if clearing her head and realizing where she was. "Yes, I'm fine." Though she answered, her features remained tight. She started to stand but Emery gripped her arm tighter, holding her in her seat.

Dana had trouble meeting her eyes and she waited until they were alone in the room. "I don't mean to pry, Dana, but are you sure you're okay?"

"I'm fine. I just have a few things on my mind."

"I hope you know you can talk to me about anything that's troubling you. Is there something going on I should know about?" She was afraid that someone in the office was giving Dana a hard time or, God forbid, James Bethel was harassing her.

Dana stiffened just before her head snapped up, fire in her eyes. "Do you think that because of our…history you have a right to my personal life?"

Her breath caught. Where in the hell had that come from?

"Because you don't," Dana said firmly. "We—"

"My only concern is your life here at Martin. That's the way it is with everyone that works for me." Her voice was harsher than she intended it to be, but Dana's reference to their "history," as she called it, had surprised her. Dana had never once alluded or even hinted about their time together. Dana never looked at her with anything other than complete professionalism. Even though that was their unspoken agreement during the cruise and their clear understanding when Dana came to work for Martin, she was surprised to discover that it hurt that Dana could so easily discard what they had shared.

Dana's anger didn't dissipate. "I said there is nothing wrong." She accentuated each word. "And if there were," she pulled her arm free of Emery's hand and stood, "I'm a big girl. I can take care of myself. I've told you that more than once."

"I'm only trying—"

"I know exactly what you're trying to do, Emery. I don't need it and I don't want it."

Dana hesitated. She might have stepped over the boundaries between boss and subordinate. She looked at her watch. "Is there anything else? I have another meeting." Her voice was softer now.

"Stupid, stupid, stupid," she said as she watched the floor numbers tick down on the elevator panel. Luckily she was alone as she rode it to the ground floor. She did have another meeting but desperately needed some fresh air. The doors opened to the spacious lobby of the building that housed the global headquarters of Martin Engineering. Her heels clicked across the marble floor, and she dodged other people coming and going through the revolving entrance door.

She squinted into the bright sun and swore under her breath because she hadn't stopped by her office to get her sunglasses. Her eyes were sensitive to the sun and constantly watered if she wasn't wearing the dark, protective Ray-Bans. Shit, now she'd look like she was crying. At least her makeup, as little as she had left, wouldn't show much damage.

She walked a few blocks to a nearby park and scanned the few benches in the shade for a place to sit down. Just her luck today, they were all occupied except for one on the far side where an elderly gentleman perched on one end.

"May I sit here?" she asked, indicating the empty space on the opposite end of the bench from the casually dressed, white-haired man. His eyes were kind when he smiled.

"Of course," he replied, and politely stood and with his hand indicated she was welcome to join him on the wooden bench.

She sat down and set her notebook and papers in the space between them, then leaned her head back and let out a long breath. What in the fuck had just happened? She had zoned out in a meeting and had no idea how a simple question from Emery had turned her into a snarling bitch.

She had been in jobs with more stress and pressure than this one and had always been able to handle it. Keeping up her exercise routine, outings with friends, and regular sexual release had always kept her sane and level-headed. Since taking this job she had managed to maintain two out of the three, but she simply had no interest in the third.

Her friends had tried to set her up and she had met some interesting, attractive women, but no one had clicked. She usually didn't need anything other than a mutual attraction for her to pursue a woman, but lately she just wasn't interested.

"Taking a break?" the man beside her asked.

"More like a time-out," she replied.

"Tough morning?"

"More like a tough few months," she said, surprising herself. She hadn't really thought about it, but her statement was spot-on.

"You work around here."

He must have based his simple statement of fact on her business suit, heels, and notebook.

"Yes." She answered vaguely. "I needed some fresh air to clear my head."

"It's the perfect day for it," the man said, not looking at her. "Not too hot, not too cool. Supposed to be just like this all week."

He continued to comment on the weather, the trees blooming, and how much rain the weatherman said they expected this summer. Dana felt herself relax listening to the benign chatter.

How had she gotten here? She was under pressure from Sharon to tattle on Emery, James Bethel still called once a week, Camille Hastings was blackmailing her to put out, and every time she looked at or even thought about Emery Barrett, her mind and knees turned to mush. Wasn't that four strikes against her? No wonder she wasn't sleeping well and had risked her job by snarling at Emery.

"Do you ever wonder if it's all worth it?" She had no idea why she'd asked the question and, even more surprising, had said it out loud. She was still looking straight ahead but could see the man turn his attention toward her for a moment before he returned his gaze to the park.

"I've been asked to be a snitch, some jerk who thinks he's God's greatest gift to women won't take no for an answer, the sister of a competitor is threatening to out me if I don't sleep with her, and I've got the hots for my boss," she said in one quick breath. "Other than that, my bills are paid, and I have a roof over my head and great friends."

"Sounds like you've got your hands full."

"No shit."

The man opened the Igloo cooler beside him, took out a bottle of water, and offered it to her. "It's unopened," he said when she looked at it. "Pretend it's a bottle of the smoothest scotch ever made. I'll leave it to your choice as to the actual distiller," he added with a soft chuckle.

"Thanks." She twisted open the lid and took several long swallows. The water was cool against her throat and immediately refreshing. Another few swallows and she began to feel much better. "Well, if I took your advice, I'd be roaring drunk by now."

"And doesn't that make the world look very different?" he replied, sipping from his own water bottle. "At least for a little while."

"How did I get into this mess? One day I'm on a sun- and fun-filled cruise with two thousand other women, the next I'm deep in this shit. I just wanted to relax and escape for a few weeks, you know? Rest, recharge, improve my tan lines, maybe meet a few interesting women. But no, I have to become involved with one particular woman, and God help me, I've fallen for her. Hard."

She had no idea why she was telling this to this total stranger. He could be anybody, and with her run of bad luck, he probably had ties to people or contacts or something else that would bite her in the butt tomorrow.

"Sounds like you should have kept your hands to yourself."

She couldn't keep from laughing. "Don't I know it." She was surprised that the man seemed to take her confession in stride.

"If you could do it all over again, would you?"

She turned her head and looked at the man. He was probably in his late seventies, had a fresh haircut and neatly trimmed beard, and wore a wedding ring. He was soft-spoken, unthreatening, and very easy to talk to. In another time she envisioned they could be friends.

She answered honestly. "Yes."

"Sounds to me like you need to figure out how you're going to get out of this mess. You're obviously bright and successful," he said, quickly surveying her suit, then looked back toward the fountain in front of them. "And you have a good head on your shoulders. You know what you need to do."

They both sat quietly for several minutes. She thought about what the man had said. He didn't pass judgment or give advice. He didn't condemn her for her choices or tell her what he thought she should do. He simply listened and lobbed the ball back into her court. Finally she glanced at her watch, shocked to see that over an hour had passed since she'd stormed out of Emery's meeting.

"I've got to go," she said, standing up. "Thank you for sharing your bench with me." She impulsively extended her hand. "Mister…"

With some effort, the man politely stood and took her hand. "Baines. Jonathon Baines."

"Thank you Mr. Baines," she said warmly, grasping his hand between both of hers. This time he looked a little lonely. "You were exactly what I needed."

"I'm here most days at this time, simply enjoying the day," he said, smiling warmly.

"Maybe I'll see you again," she said, realizing that she meant the sometimes-empty comment. She gathered her things and set off back toward her office, still not clear about what she would do but more determined than ever to figure it out.

Chapter Twenty-three

I'll leave you two powerful executives to talk while I go and be a simple mommy," Lauren said, taking Grace from Dana's arms. Dana had invited herself over for dinner, and she and Elliott were sitting on the patio enjoying an unusually warm evening. She still couldn't believe that Grace was already four months old. Where did the time go?

"You're very lucky, Elliott."

"And I thank God every day," Elliott said, lifting her feet to rest on the chaise lounge.

"You have a great job, a beautiful baby, and a woman who loves you as much today as she did the first day you met." Dana was envious.

"I wouldn't go that far. Lauren hated me the first time we met." Elliott took a sip of her drink.

"She was just playing hard to get," she replied. They both laughed.

"And she did a great job. I had to chase her until she caught me." Elliott twirled the wide gold band on her left hand.

"Is being the head of Foster McKenzie everything you'd thought it would be?" Elliott was the CEO of the company her father had built and her uncle had almost destroyed.

"Sometimes it's more and sometimes it's less. It depends on the day and the situation. But overall I'd say yes."

"Do you ever just want to walk away and say to hell with it and its constraints?"

"Same answer."

She sipped on the fresh cocktail Lauren had given her a few minutes before taking Grace and leaving them alone on the patio.

"Have you ever been torn in different directions? Conflicted as to what you should do, you know, in something really big? Something that could ruin you professionally."

Elliott shifted in her chair. "What's going on, Dana? Is something wrong at Martin?"

"Dana?" Lauren's voice was filled with concern as she stepped out onto the deck. Elliott moved her feet and Lauren sat down facing her.

"You'll never guess." She shook her head. She hardly believed it herself.

"Emery made a pass at you," Lauren said, frowning. "I'm going to kick her ass if she hurts you."

She knew Lauren would do it too. "No, she didn't." She emphasized the word *she* but Lauren didn't notice.

Elliott guessed. "Somebody knows about you two."

"Are you in some kind of trouble?" Lauren leaned forward and laid a comforting hand on her leg.

"Yes and no." This time Elliott sat forward.

"Do you two want me to leave?"

If she was in legal trouble she could discuss it with Lauren under the protection of the attorney-client privilege. Lauren couldn't disclose anything she said without running the risk of losing her license to practice law. Elliott, however, did not benefit from that same cloak of confidentiality.

"No, Elliott, please stay. I value your input and point of view."

"You're making me nervous, Dana. Tell us what's going on."

She spent the next forty minutes describing the shit that had piled up around her. They asked a few clarifying questions along the way but basically let her go at her own pace. She was furious as she recalled the conversations with Sharon Plenner, disgusted describing Jim Bethel, and almost detached when she detailed the incident with Camille Hastings. She told them how she'd lost it with Emery earlier today and about her conversation with the sweet old man at the park. By the time she was done she was exhausted.

"Wow," Elliott said simply.

"I'll kill her if she hurts you…that other woman…what was her name…Hastings?" Lauren said forcefully.

"Lauren," Elliott said.

"I'm just spouting off." Lauren sighed loudly. "I have to get my emotions out before I can think clearly on this one."

"Too bad," Dana said sarcastically. "That would take care of one of my problems."

"What are you going to do?" Elliott looked perturbed

"I don't know. Bethel is a pest and I'm going to tell him to take a hike. I told Sharon I would not be her pipeline and have been dodging her ever since. I'm worried, though, about what she might do to Emery."

"Are you going to tell Emery about her?" This time Lauren asked.

"She probably already knows," Elliott said. "If Emery is as sharp as you say she is, Dana, and as astute as everything I've read about her, she already knows who's in her camp and who's waiting on the sidelines stoking the fire."

"But what if she doesn't? She has a right to know."

"Then tell her," Lauren said simply.

She nodded several times, knowing it would be a difficult conversation but one she had to have with Emery. She cared too much to see her get blindsided and her reputation sullied by the likes of Sharon.

"What are you going to do about Camille Hastings?"

"I have no fucking clue. She's got me by the short hairs—no pun intended." She chuckled. "If I don't do what she wants she'll tell the Feds. I won't be the cause of Emery's downfall."

"If you do what she wants she may still tell," Elliott said carefully. "Industrial blackmail is nothing to take lightly, and that's exactly what she's doing. Do you really think she'll just forget about what she saw, or hand over the pictures she has of you and Emery? This is the digital age…they are forever."

"Elliott." Lauren began to chastise her.

"No, Lauren," Elliott said, turning quickly to face her. "Dana needs to hear this. I know what I'm talking about." Elliott redirected her attention to Dana. "Trust me. The Camille Hastingses of the world will not stop at one time. She will hold this over your head for the rest of your life, or until she believes her information is no longer valuable."

Elliott took Dana's hands in hers. "You are my wife's best friend, and along with that comes my love and commitment to your welfare and happiness. I can help you."

Elliott's statement hung in the air. Lauren stared at Elliott as if she had just discovered something frightening about the woman who'd shared her life all these years. Dana instinctively knew what Elliott was talking about and didn't want to put her or Lauren in the middle of this. "No, Elliott."

"Let me help you, Dana," Elliott said softly.

"I can't." Dana despised the quiver in her voice.

"Why not?"

She didn't answer but simply looked between Lauren and Elliott. Lauren's expression was her answer. Suddenly she stood.

"Dana, I am your friend and an attorney, and as an attorney I am bound to uphold and report any violations of the law that I am aware of. You are my best friend and one of the three people I love more than life itself. And as your friend I'm telling you that I will always be your friend first and your attorney second. Now, if you two ladies will excuse me, I think I hear the baby."

She sat stunned at Lauren's words. "Did she just do what I think she did?" Elliott nodded but didn't say anything. "Did she just disavow any knowledge of anything we do to Camille Hastings?" Elliott nodded again.

"God, I love that woman."

She and Elliott talked for several hours, and when she left it was close to midnight. She had declined Lauren's offer of the guest room and drove home much more optimistic about her future.

Chapter Twenty-four

Camille, come in," Dana said as she closed the door behind her well-dressed blackmailer. "Please, sit down, won't you?"

Camille Hastings glanced around the large office before settling into one of the chairs across from Dana's desk.

"Nice suit," Camille commented, after setting her purse on the floor and crossing her legs.

"Thank you." Dana had taken extra care with her appearance this morning. She was wearing what she called her "don't fuck with me" suit, and she felt fabulous and confident. "I won't offer you something to drink," she said pleasantly, sitting deep in the leather chair behind her large desk. "You won't be here that long."

Camille replied smugly. "Really."

"Yes, really. I suppose you're wondering why I asked to meet you here...in my office...just down the hall from Emery's office... in the *headquarters* of Martin Engineering?" She paused during her question, for maximum effect.

"I will admit I expected our next conversation to be...how shall I put it...in a more *intimate* surrounding."

Her skin crawled as Camille's eyes crudely settled on her breasts and she licked her lips.

"Then let me enlighten you, Camille. You are here because you don't scare me. You and your threats are nothing to me. Who do you think you are, threatening me? Do you think I'm some little chippie you can scare into sleeping with you? Do I look that stupid? Do I look like I have shit for brains?" Her confidence soared at Camille's shocked expression. Elliott had prepared her well.

"How many other women have you pulled this crap on? Oh, no, wait." She held up her hand, as if to stop Camille from answering even if she could. "Let me answer my own question." She ticked the names off on her fingers. "Let's see there were Joan, Rebecca, Carol." She paused. The spark of fear in Camille's eyes told her she had made her point. "Do I need to continue? You know I can."

Camille shook her head and said nothing. Her once-rosy complexion was now quite pale and her jaw so slack her mouth was almost open. *Thank you, Elliott.*

"I didn't think so. Now let me tell you something." She had yet to raise her voice or even uncross her legs. "If you ever dare to threaten me, Emery, or anyone else I love again, you will have me to answer to. And if you're thinking about mentioning this to your brother, just ask him about Tidewater. I'm sure he'll be able to change your mind." She dropped the name of the company Elliott had given her, along with the information as to what exactly Bethel had to hide regarding his dealings with the manufacturer. "And let me assure you, I can dump more shit on you than you can even begin to imagine. Now take your Botox face, fake boobs, and pathetic little threats and get out of my office."

Yes, Elliott had indeed prepared her well.

C<small>HAPTER</small> T<small>WENTY</small>-<small>FIVE</small>

"Emery?" Dana asked, standing in the doorway of her office. Emery looked up. "You got a minute? I'd like to talk to you about something." She was glad that her voice didn't seem to mimic the butterflies dancing around in her stomach. She had tried to eat lunch an hour ago, but her stomach wouldn't let her.

"Sure, come on in." Emery placed her pen on the stack of papers in front of her and indicated the chair across from her desk.

A look of apprehension flashed in Emery's eyes when she closed the door behind her. She was too keyed up to sit down. Emery must have picked up on her nervousness about starting the conversation she had practiced all morning. This one would be far more difficult than the one she'd had with Camille three days earlier.

"What is it?"

"Sharon Plenner approached me and asked me to spy on you."

Emery didn't immediately respond but looked at her hard. She felt as if she were being dissected and Emery was deciding whether to trust what she had to say next.

"When?"

"The first time was shortly after I started."

"The *first* time?" Emery asked quickly.

"Yes." She began to feel like a traitor for not telling Emery as soon as Sharon made her initial move. "She's approached me several times."

"I see," Emery said.

She hadn't expected Emery's calm reply. Actually she hadn't known how Emery would react, but it certainly wasn't this cool, almost-detached demeanor. Unsettled, she continued.

"She said she was looking for someone to help keep Martin on the right track, as she phrased it."

"And what did you say?"

"I told her no," she said firmly. Emery's expression didn't change. "I said I was uncomfortable with the conversation and that if she had a problem with you, she needed to deal with it through proper board channels."

Emery rubbed her eyes and simply nodded.

"She didn't vote for you."

"I know."

Elliott was right. Emery did know what was going on with her board members. "She's fishing for information about your leave." Emery's eyes narrowed and something dangerous flashed in them.

"What did you tell her?" Emery's voice was cold.

Her gut clenched. Did Emery actually think she would tell Sharon? Did she think she would give Sharon any information she could use as ammunition? They might have pretended to be total strangers, but didn't Emery know her better than that?

"Nothing." She wasn't sure if Emery sighed with relief or simply took a deep breath.

"Thank you."

"For what?" she asked, her nerves giving way to anger. "For not ratting on you, my boss, the woman who has given me a chance to help make this company successful? Not agreeing to spy on you and report back to the likes of Sharon Plenner? Not using our time together on the ship as a means of bringing you to your knees? Not defiling what we had by becoming a traitor to what we shared?" She stopped, suddenly aware she was close to losing control.

"For confirming what I suspected," Emery replied coolly. "It was pretty clear that Sharon didn't want me for this job. She hates the fact that I'm a lesbian and can't get past it." Emery rose from her chair, looked out the window, and straightened her back.

"I have taken this company from the brink of disaster, with zero shareholder value, to a market cap of over eighteen billion and

complete and utter respectability in half the time they gave me."
Emery chuckled, turning around to face her.

"I just got word this morning that Martin is officially off the
government watch list. There will be no more sanctions or second
looks at our practices. We are preparing a press release, and when it
hits the street, our stock will skyrocket. And Sharon Plenner is more
concerned about who I have sex with than the millions of dollars I
have made our investors, her included." Emery shook her head and
put her hands in her pockets.

"It's people like her that make me want to throw it all away and
do something completely different. But I don't. You know why?"

She knew it was a rhetorical question and sat quietly waiting.

"Because of people like Lars Calhoun in accounting, who worked
ninety-hour weeks trying to do the right thing. It's for David Sandling
in purchasing, who missed his daughter's first birthday because the
fracture project was due the next day. It's because of the dozens of
people who called in to the ethics hotline to help clean up the shit this
company was oozing."

Emery turned and looked at her, and she felt the intensity of
Emery's position. She also felt petty and embarrassed by her self-
centered thought. "It's because of people like you who refuse to do
anything but the right thing."

"Now if you'll excuse me I have some calls to make," Emery
said, effectively dismissing Dana. She had to get her out of her office
before she fell apart. Her hands were in her pockets so Dana couldn't
see how badly they were shaking. She had to pace or she'd faint. What
Dana had told her had completely thrown her world into a tailspin and
she had to fight to keep it from crashing—at least in front of Dana.

Dana pulled the door closed behind her and she stumbled into her
chair. Her head was swimming and she fought back the nausea that
threatened to make her throw up. She'd known Sharon was trouble
and suspected she had gone as far as to try to cultivate an insider. As
far as she could tell Sharon hadn't succeeded, and Dana's revelation
confirmed it.

She hadn't lied to Dana. Lately she had been having more
thoughts about moving on. She could now. She had completed her
mission. Martin was once again a good, corporate citizen and, thanks

to her own confidence, she had negotiated a very large bonus if this happened before the end of five years.

She swiveled her chair and once again looked out her window. Martin was months ahead of schedule, and she was going to be a very wealthy woman. But that didn't matter to her. She already had enough money. There would be articles written about her, the *Harvard Business Review* was already chronicling her achievements and planned to use this turnaround in one of their published case studies. Emery Barrett would be an even more familiar name in business across the world. Going forward she could have her pick of opportunities. They were already starting to come in. Executive headhunters called her several times a week, trying to lure her away with offers of complete control, an open checkbook, and tens of millions of dollars in her bank account. But she wasn't interested in any of them. She had a job to do at Martin and had been committed to finishing it. And now it was done.

The stars were high in the sky when she turned her chair back around. She heard the cleaning crew in the outer office and was surprised when her clock read seven thirty-four. Dana had entered her office just after lunch, and by some quirk of luck she had not been interrupted for the remainder of the day. She made a note to thank Adam.

Ignoring her briefcase and the stack of colored folders on her desk, she picked up her wallet and keys, said good night to the lady emptying Adam's trash can, and stepped into the empty elevator.

Chapter Twenty-six

"What's on your mind, Emery?" Julia asked after filling Emery's wineglass. They were sitting outside on Julia's patio, a blanket covering their legs, an empty wine bottle on the table in front of them. "We've talked about the weather, my patients, my new car, and the new neighbors down the street. All important, yet superficial crap."

She looked at Julia. She thought about lying, but Julia was her best friend and sometimes knew her better than she knew herself, so that was out of the question.

She had no idea how to answer that question. She liked Dana, respected her, even admired her. But was that professional or personal? She knew Dee, but connecting her to the Dana in the office was a blur. She was having too many sleepless nights again, this time due to Dana. And when she did finally fall asleep she dreamed of her. She'd been debating whether to confide in Julia but then Julia's phone had rung. She'd been relieved when Julia had to dash off to the hospital because if she herself hadn't figured it out, how would she talk to Julia about it?

Now Julia was back, sitting upright and leaning on the edge of the couch cushions. "Does this have anything to do with Dana?"

Emery must have had her thoughts on her sleeve because Julia immediately snapped her fingers, pointed at her, and said, "I knew it." She settled back on the couch and crossed her legs. "Okay, spill. I let you get away with not telling me anything about her when you put her in charge of that acquisition. But now I want every single detail. Especially if you're still thinking about her."

She fought the need to get up and move. Or was it to get up and run? She had no idea what to say to Julia and she told her as much.

"Bullshit," Julia said. "I've known you for over twenty years and I've never seen you at a loss for words. Just open your mouth and it'll all come tumbling out."

She wanted to tell Julia. God, she had to talk to someone about it, other than herself. She wasn't much help to herself, and she certainly needed someone, especially after Dana had stormed out of her office last week. Julia kept silent.

"I need to have my head examined," she said. "Dana is everything I knew she would be. She's by far one of the best people I've ever hired."

"And?"

"And I can't get her out of my mind, or out from under my skin," she added dryly. "She's all I think about. I mean not just when I'm at home or have some free time, but almost every second of the day I'm not unconscious. If she's in the room with me, in a meeting or something, I can't concentrate and I can't take my eyes off her. If she's not, then I'm wondering where she is and what she's doing. I'm constantly getting caught not paying attention, and even my staff is starting to look at me as if I'm losing my mind. I feel like I have mush for brains." This time she didn't fight the need to get up and move around.

"I'm distracted, unfocused, and in worse condition than I was before I went on that stupid cruise. Jesus, I was supposed to relax, not get all wrapped around some woman who then comes to work for me." She sat down again, feeling like a jack-in-the-box. "What a cluster fuck my life has become." She dropped her head into her hands and ran her fingers through her hair.

"I'm happy for you."

"What?" she asked, not sure she'd heard Julia correctly.

"I said I'm happy for you. Admit it, Emery. You have effectively cruised through life skirting any chance of being bitten by the lovebug. Or even the smitten bug. You're thirty-eight years old and have never had a serious relationship with a woman. You've never let yourself get that close. You hit-and-run women."

"Hit and run?"

"Yes. You don't stop long enough to exchange anything important with a woman except her phone number and how many times you can make her come in one night."

"That's not true!" she said defensively.

"Honey, you can bullshit me and you can lie to yourself, but I'm your best friend and with that comes the ability to see right through you. Now, I love you and wouldn't do anything to intentionally hurt you, but I'm telling you the truth. And you know it."

She didn't say anything. Julia was right. Rarely had she given any woman more than a few hours or, in several rare cases, more than a few days of her attention. She was focused on her career and needed her relationships to be brief, easy, and unencumbered. If the women she met met those criteria, they would spend time together with nothing more than pleasant, if fleeting memories. If not, she quickly moved on.

But where did Dana fit in? That was the problem. She didn't *fit* anywhere. The time she had spent with Dee had been brief, easy, and unencumbered. Her relationship with Dana, however, was anything but. It was urgent, emotional, unsettling, consuming, demanding, and like nothing she had ever experienced before. She was completely out of her element.

"I'm not in love with her," she said, surprised at how shaky her voice was.

"I didn't say you were," Julia said calmly. "I'm just saying that from where I sit you're all messed up over this woman. It's bad enough you can't get her out of your head, but that, plus the stress of getting caught pulling your hand out of the proverbial cookie jar, is making you crazy."

"My hand is not in her cookie jar," Emery said.

Julia looked at her, sighed, and rolled her eyes. "You are such an engineer, so exact and precise. You know what I'm talking about."

"So what am I supposed to do?" she asked, mentally exhausted.

Julia emptied the wine bottle into their glasses. "I'm afraid I can't help you with that one."

"What kind of friend are you?" Emery asked, feigning fear.

"One who will listen to you bitch and complain, be your sounding board, and offer my two cents' worth of advice. In other words...the best kind."

Chapter Twenty-seven

When would her hands stop shaking? They shook as she gripped the steering wheel, when she locked the car, and when she tried to push the doorbell. While she waited Emery remembered the end of the cruise.

Tomorrow it would be over. The sense of contentment EJ felt with Dee in her arms frightened her. This trip, this woman was unlike anything she had ever experienced. Why was it so different this time? She had had brief affairs before, but none left her with a sense of dread when it was time to leave. She wanted to see Dee again, wanted to ask her for her phone number, take her to dinner at her favorite restaurant, eat pizza in bed and watch Humphrey Bogart movies. If she was lucky Dee lived on the other side of the country, which would make the continuation of this relationship difficult at best. With her luck Dee probably lived on the next street over in her neighborhood.

But that wasn't part of their deal. They had both agreed that when the ship docked their affair was over. Their sex these last few days was almost extreme, a force so powerful neither one of them could get enough of each other. Last night their lovemaking reflected the realization that this would be the last time they would kiss, touch, feel each other's bodies join in the dark. Even after hours of demanding kisses, insistent caresses, and breathless release, she'd barely slept. She'd wanted to savor and memorize every moment with Dee. After Dee walked out of her suite, her life would never be the same again.

An instant of panic seized Emery. What was she doing here, at Dana's front door at midnight? But then she remembered how it felt just being with her. It was more than the sex. She felt alive, interesting, challenged, thought of, and cherished. She didn't have to impress Dana or be anyone but herself with her. Other than Julia she had no one else like that. That used to be okay, but no longer. She'd let Dana get away the first time. The second time would kill her.

"Emery?"

Her heart jumped at the sight of Dana standing in front of her. One hand clasped the edges of a silk robe together, and the other ran through her hair. It was obvious she had been sleeping.

"What is it?" Dana asked again. "Has something happened?"

She didn't allow herself to think. She'd done enough thinking to last a lifetime. She wanted to feel. For once in her life she wanted to do what she *wanted* to do, not what she *should* do. But with Dana this wasn't what she wanted, it was what she needed to do. There were no second thoughts, no doubts, no hesitation.

She stepped forward, intending to kiss Dana. Then she lifted her gaze from Dana's lips to her eyes and saw surprise.

"Emery, what are you doing?"

Slowly, savoring the anticipation, she lowered her head and lightly kissed Dana. Her lips were softer than she remembered and the kiss made her head spin.

She fought the urge to pull Dana to her and smother her with kisses. She wanted Dana so badly it hurt. Kissing her felt like she had come home. Funny, she thought, she'd never realized she was anywhere but home. To hell with convention, this was so right. How had she ever thought her life was complete without this? Without Dana?

Dana slowly responded and kissed her back. Tentative at first, Dana's desire soon turned into much more. Their tongues dueled, fighting for control, surrendering to pleasure.

Suddenly Dana pulled away, her hand at her mouth. "Have you lost your mind?" She looked around and behind Emery, as if expecting the flash of cameras in the darkness.

"No," she replied, her eyes never leaving Dana's. "I remember everything. I remember how you loved me. I remember your touch, your scent, your taste. I remember how time stood still when I was with you. I remember how it felt to fall asleep in your arms and wake up to your touch. I remember the way you knew just what I needed. I remember making love under the moon. I remember every moment we spent together. And I want to have more than just memories. Something's going on between us. I can't think, I can't concentrate, I can hardly breathe without you. It scares me to death to feel this way, but I can't live any other way. I don't want to. I've been so lost without you. I don't want to be lonely anymore. I won't survive losing you again."

Emery's words slid around Dana's heart. It was as if they were reading off the same page in a book. Emery's words had been scripted from her own heart.

Emery's eyes, hungry with desire, exposed her deepest thoughts and fears. Emery was offering herself, all of her, risking everything for her.

She didn't need any more conversation. Words couldn't convey what she was feeling. She only needed Emery in her arms. She took Emery's hand, pulled her through the door, and threw the deadbolt. As she stood there watching Emery she had a moment of panic.

"You could lose everything."

"I don't care."

"Martin—"

"Will be fine."

"But—"

"But nothing. I've already let you go once, I'm not going to let it happen again." She had come too far, had too much at stake to stop now. This time when she kissed Dana she wasn't gentle but demanding. To her joy and relief, Dana's response was just as powerful.

Dana broke the kiss only to take her hand and lead her upstairs. She stopped and turned around when Emery didn't follow.

"Emery?"

Dana was two steps above her, her body shadowed by the light in the hall. "You are so beautiful."

"I've waited so long to hear you say that again." Dana's voice was soft and sensuous. This wasn't her nine-to-five voice, and Emery had thought she would forever hear it only in her dreams. After months of anxiety and edginess, she was finally calm and slowly followed Dana to her bedroom. A lone lamp beside the bed cast the room in a soft, romantic glow. Dana had thrown back the covers on one side of the bed when she had gotten up to answer the door. Like on the cruise, she slept on the left side of the bed.

Dana went to the other side of the bed and pulled back the other side, exposing deep-red sheets. She lay down in the center and waited.

Emery knew Dana was giving her a choice, but ever since she'd seen Dana on that deck the first day of the cruise she'd had no choice. She had always scoffed at sappy romantic phrases, things like she was a vision, a soothing cloth to her parched existence. But suddenly they all made sense. That was what people said when they were in love. The world looked different, brighter, cleaner, purer when you were in love. Words like crave, yearn, and ache were now real.

Dana held out her hand. With each step toward her, Emery gave a little more of herself. Why had it taken so long for them to get here? Logically Dana knew why, but her body told her it had been a complete waste of time. Dana was speechless. She had never heard anything as poetic in her life as Emery's declaration. Emery had held her in the palm of her hand and taken her to immeasurable heights. Not wanting to squander any more of their precious moments together, she pulled Emery into her bed.

Shock waves of delight coursed through her every nerve ending. At this moment, she knew they would be together forever. They would have tough times, but Emery would never leave her. She was too good, too decent to take the easy way out. They'd started the cruise as separate individuals and were now one.

Her body heated when Emery kissed her and explored her mouth with her tongue as if it were undiscovered territory. Her hands were busy too, and Dana quivered when Emery stroked her face, her neck, her shoulders. Emery's familiar weight pressed on her.

Emery's mouth slowly followed the trail of her hands and she could only gasp as warm, wet lips circled her nipple. It grew harder, and with each flick of Emery's tongue Dana slid one stroke closer to orgasm. Emery knew her body like no other lover and exploited that knowledge to the fullest.

Finally she couldn't take it any more. "Emery, love, touch me, please. I need you now, fast and hard. It's been too long. I don't want to wait. I can't wait. Please." At this point she had no pride. She'd never begged for anything but she would beg for Emery to let her do this. She needed it now, couldn't wait for the preliminaries or the removal of clothes. She had to touch Emery, breathe in her scent, taste her come.

The time for making love would be later, much later. What she needed now was to feel Emery inside her driving her to climax. She needed to release, to explode, completely lose control in the safety of Emery's arms. She didn't have to ask twice.

Dana's cry of surrender echoed off the walls and Emery couldn't hold back her own orgasm. The sensation of Dana willingly giving herself and coming in her arms like this overwhelmed her.

Dana's body was a wonderland of peaks and valleys, curves and soft angles she could explore forever, but right now she was content with Dana quivering from aftershocks in her arms. Her life was now complete. An overwhelming sense of rightness settled over her. She and Dana had been in this exact position many times before, but it never felt like this. Before, they had been intimate strangers, purely physical, merely sharing their bodies freely.

"This feels like the first time," she said softly. She was still inside Dana and felt her tighten around her fingers.

"Hardly," Dana said breathlessly. Emery held her tighter. After several more minutes she slid her fingers out of Dana's warmth and cupped her. She lifted her head and looked at Dana. "Open your eyes."

"I don't think I can."

She flicked her thumb over Dana's clit.

Dana inhaled sharply. "That's not going to help," she said breathlessly.

"If you want me to do it again you'll open your eyes and look at me. After another few seconds she did. Emery could barely see, residual passion clouding her eyes.

"Not fair," Dana said.

Emery sat up and looked down at Dana lying spent and naked on her bed. A fine sheen of sweat covered her flushed skin. "You are the most beautiful woman in the world. You're smart, funny, intriguing, and very, very sexy. I want to spend the rest of my life seeing you just like this. I want to go to sleep with you in my arms every night. I want to argue with you and have hot make-up sex with you. I want to hold your head when you're sick and your hand on the beach. I want to get a puppy with you and introduce you to my mom. I love you, Dana Worthington."

Dana sat up and kissed Emery, pushing her onto her back. "Now it's my turn to show you just how much I love you."

"I can't say no to you, Dana," Emery said, her voice hitching with desire.

❖

Much, much later Emery dozed as the ceiling fan rotated overhead, cooling the sweat that coated their skin. "God, I've missed you," she said. Dana was back in her arms where she belonged. Life was perfect.

"You see me practically every day," Dana replied, tweaking her nipple.

"Hey." She swatted Dana's hand away. "That's not what I meant. I've missed you—in my life. I remember the first time I saw you."

"Tell me."

"It was on deck, when we left Ft. Lauderdale."

"Really? I thought you would have said that at dinner the first night."

"No. I remember seeing you standing by yourself and wondering why your girlfriend wasn't with you on deck. I thought she was a fool for letting a woman as beautiful as you alone at such a romantic and exciting time."

Dana leaned up, bracing herself on her elbows. "I had no idea you were such a romantic."

"Neither did I until I met you." She couldn't believe how true that statement actually was. She didn't think she was the kind of woman who was moved by time, place, and ambience. Sure, she did all the right things, said all the right words, but those actions came from her head, not her heart. Dana had her heart and she prayed Dana never let go.

"Do you remember what I said to Jim Bethel when you introduced me?"

She remembered practically every word Dana said, but Dana didn't give her a chance to answer.

"I said, 'When I'm through with Emery, you'll be the first one I call.'"

She chuckled. "God, yes, it was perfect. He had no idea what you were talking about."

Dana sat up and moved on top of her. This was her favorite position—Dana above her, where she could watch her completely. Dana started to move against her, and her pulse began to pound again.

"Well, he's in for a very long wait because I'll never be through with you."

"God, I hope not," she managed to say just before Dana's mouth closed over hers.

This time, as they caught their breath, she slid her hands over Dana's muscular arms. "Did you swim when you were a little girl?" She had an image of what Dana might have looked like as a child—and what their child might look like.

"I was on the swim team every summer through high school."

"Why the chuckle?" she asked.

"When I was seventeen a new girl, Shannon Bell, joined the team. She spent the rest of the summer trying to get me out of the pool and out of my suit."

It was her turn to laugh. "Did she succeed?"

"Did she ever. If I'd known what it was like to be with a woman I'd have said yes even before she asked."

"Your first time?" she asked, realizing this was their first personal pillow talk.

"And my second and fourth and fiftieth," Dana said, amused. "We were together all summer."

"Taught you everything you know, did she?"

"Nope, but enough to get started. It ended when I had to go to college."

For the second time in as many hours Dana slid on top of her, their legs intertwining as if they were made that way. "She taught me this." Dana lightly nipped at her breast. "And this." She licked the nipple with the flat of her tongue. "And this," she added as she slid her finger into Emery's hot core.

"Remind me to thank her," she said, quickly losing track of who they were even talking about.

Chapter Twenty-eight

Hello, Emery? Where are you?"

Adam's voice pulled her out of her daydreams about night things. To be precise, exactly thirty-two nights of things she and Dana shared.

"Don't give me that 'I don't know what you're talking about' look. You forget that I know everything about you."

Not everything, she thought. "Just taking a trip down memory lane."

"Well, by the look on your face it's X-rated."

She laughed. "Well, then, Dr. Freud, since you know so much about coitus interruptus, what do you want?"

"Sharon Plenner is here."

"Show her in."

"Do you want me to buzz you?" When Adam had first come to work for her they'd devised a code that he would buzz Emery as an escape route if she thought she might need it.

"No, she won't be here that long."

She straightened her suit jacket as Sharon entered her office. "Thanks for coming, Sharon," she said, not giving any indication she was welcome to sit. Sharon did anyway.

"I don't take it kindly to being summoned. You work for the board, remember?" She didn't say but was probably thinking, "and therefore you work for me."

"Well, I don't take kindly to you trying to turn my staff against me." Sharon started to say something but she cut her off. "Don't bother to deny it. I know all about it and everyone you've approached." She stood, walked around her desk, and sat on the edge. "You've never liked me, and frankly I don't care. The board didn't hire me to be your friend. This is a business, not a social club."

"You can't talk to me like that."

"Yes, Sharon, I can, and I'm not finished. You're a poor excuse for a board member of the largest, most successful independent engineering firm in the world. You should be touting Martin to everyone in the industry, even suggesting that our success was due to your leadership on the board. You could advance yourself and Martin light years ahead of our nearest competitor.

"But you've been too busy with your personal agenda against me. In case you haven't read up on it, being a lesbian isn't something you can catch. It's who you are or who you are not. Who someone chooses to love has nothing to do with how well they do their job, and who I choose to love has nothing to do with how well I do mine." She hesitated, allowing time for her words to sink in. "Wait, I take that back. Maybe it does. Wasn't it a group of male heterosexuals that drove this company into the ground?

"Now if you'll excuse me," she said, walking across her office and opening the door. "I have a business to run."

When Sharon stood and turned around, whatever she had planned to say died on her lips as she came face to face with Marcus Flowers, chairman of the board of Martin Engineering.

"How'd it go?" Dana asked several hours later when Emery entered her office.

"Just as I expected. People like Sharon are all the same. Full of threats and intimation and hot air, but when you hold their feet to the fire they tumble like a house of cards."

"How are you?" Dana asked in a tone that made Emery's knees weak.

She sat down in the chair across from her. "Wanting you again."

When they were on the ship they were insatiable for each other. But that was pure lust. This was very different. This was the all-consuming, head-over-heels, overwhelming need to be with the one you love.

"I could close my door," Dana replied.

She stood and walked toward the door before she did something stupid. "Yes, you could and you wouldn't get any argument out of me. But I don't think that's a good idea. Besides, I have a meeting in fifteen minutes."

"It wouldn't take more than five," Dana said suggestively.

She laughed, her pulse pounding between her legs. "That, Ms. Worthington, I have absolutely no doubt of. I'll hold you to it later."

Dana was still smiling when the phone rang an hour later.

"Hey, Dana, it's Elliott."

"Elliott, hi," she said, surprised. Elliott had only called her at her office a handful of times, all of them centering on something to do with Lauren.

"Have you got a minute?"

"Sure, what's up?"

"I have a business proposition for you.'

"Okay…"

"Foster McKenzie is buying a company that is in desperate need of a new CEO. I think you'd be perfect for the job."

"Excuse me," Dana said, not quite sure she'd heard Elliott correctly.

"Look, I know you haven't been at Martin very long. If you're tied to them by contract or something I can wait. I really do think you'd be perfect for this job."

"Elliott, I'm stunned. I don't know what to say." Stunned was hardly the word. Shell-shocked, afraid, thrilled, excited also came to mind.

"I know I caught you off guard. I'm not expecting you to give me an answer right now. Think about it. Why don't you come over this weekend and we'll talk about it some more. I know Lauren would love to see you, and Grace is growing so fast you'd hardly recognize her. Please, Dana, I'm just asking you to think about it."

She hung up the receiver and noticed her hands shaking. What had just happened? Had Elliott called and offered her the chance to run her own company? And what a wonderful opportunity, under the guidance of a CEO of Elliott's caliber. Like Emery, Elliott had saved Foster McKenzie from certain failure. She could learn so much from

Elliott. God, she could learn so much from Emery and Elliott. She'd worked under several exceptional leaders and had toiled under several crappy ones. She had seen the bad and learned from the good. She realized she was ready to take that experience and put it into practice.

Suddenly it dawned on her that this would be the solution to the situation that she and Emery now found themselves. They couldn't go on being as involved as they were, as much in love as they were without someone finding out. They had talked about it long into the night last night, between passionate kisses and quivering desire. They'd decided not to make any rash decisions. Neither of them was willing to give up her position or ask the other to do the same. So they decided not to do anything, at least for now.

The press release with the news that Martin was no longer on the watch list had been released this morning, and Martin's stock had soared. Martin was on the right track, back as the premier engineering-design company. They both knew what needed to be done to mitigate any chance of Martin falling under the shadows again.

This would work, she thought again. But she didn't know where this company was. It could be based in Switzerland and she would have to move. It could be based in California and she could commute. She was grasping at straws and lifted the phone again.

After talking to Lauren and confirming a time to visit the coming weekend, she walked down the hall to Emery's office and peered through the doorway. Emery was on the phone, but she motioned her in before she had a chance to step back.

As Emery finished her call, Dana closed the door and looked around the office. She'd been in this office dozens of times, had looked at the plaques honoring Emery and her service to the industry, to the community. She was always envious, always proud, and never jealous of Emery's success. The phone call from Elliott had opened a door and she was ready.

"Hey, there," Emery said after hanging up the phone, her tone warm.

"Hey there yourself." She sat down in her favorite chair in front of the desk.

There must have been an unusual look on her face because Emery asked cautiously, "What's up?"

She noted the subtle signs of stress around Emery's eyes as she spoke. "Um…I got an interesting phone call from a friend of mine a little while ago."

Emery didn't say anything, just sat quietly waiting for her to continue.

"Um, remember I told you about Lauren, my best friend?"

"The one who had the baby a few months ago?"

"Yea, uh…her partner is Elliott Foster." She waited for Emery to recognize the name.

"Yeah." Dana nodded. "*That* Elliott Foster."

"Wow, if I knew you hung out in such celebrity company I'd have invited myself over for dinner."

She detected that Emery was nervous. "Yeah, um, Elliott called and she um…Foster McKenzie is acquiring a company and she asked me if I'd consider being the CEO." She watched Emery's expression change from shock to fear to pride.

"Dana, that's wonderful," Emery said, and Dana knew she meant it.

"Thanks, but I haven't given her an answer. Actually I don't know much more than that. She invited me over this weekend to talk about it some more and of course to see the baby."

Emery pursed her lips and nodded. "I don't know what to say."

She quickly stood, walked around the desk, and turned Emery's chair until they faced each other. She had her hands on the plush leather arms, bringing their faces inches apart.

"I don't know what this is, Emery. I don't know anything about it. I don't know where the company is or what they do. But I love you, and I won't do anything to jeopardize what we have together."

"Dana, I think you should—"

"No," she replied strongly. "I don't want to hear what you think I should do. I'll say it one more time and as many times as I have to until you believe me. I love you, Emery Barrett, and I will not do anything to jeopardize what we have with each other. I plan to spend the rest of my life with you. I plan to grow old with you. I plan to have children with you, and I refuse to do anything to put that at risk. So I suggest you take a deep breath, relax, and kiss me, because I have to go back to work."

"Strong, decisive, clear, articulate, passionate, visionary." Emery ticked off the attributes on her fingers. "Spoken like a true CEO," Emery said, just before she kissed her.

The End

About the Author

Julie Cannon divides her time by being a corporate suit, a partner, mom, sister, friend, and writer. Julie and Laura, her partner of twenty-one years, have lived in at least a half a dozen states, and have an unending supply of dedicated friends. And of course the most important people in their lives are their thirteen-year-old son and twelve-year-old daughter.

Julie has nine books published by Bold Strokes Books. Her first novel, *Come and Get Me*, was a finalist for the Golden Crown Literary Society's Best Lesbian Romance and Debut Author Awards. In 2012, her ninth novel, *Rescue Me*, was a finalist as Best Lesbian Romance from the prestigious Lambda Literary Society. Julie has also published five short stories in Bold Strokes anthologies.

Books Available from Bold Strokes Books

Desolation Point by Cari Hunter. When a storm strands Sarah Kent in the North Cascades, Alex Pascal is determined to find her. Neither imagines the dangers they will face when a ruthless criminal begins to hunt them down. (978-1-60282-865-0)

I Remember by Julie Cannon. What happens when you can never forget the first kiss, the first touch, the first taste of lips on skin? What happens when you know you will remember every single detail of a mysterious woman? (978-1-60282-866-7)

The Gemini Deception by Kim Baldwin and Xenia Alexiou. The truth, the whole truth, and nothing but lies. Book six in the Elite Operatives series. (978-1-60282-867-4)

Scarlet Revenge by Sheri Lewis Wohl. When faith alone isn't enough, will the love of one woman be strong enough to save a vampire from damnation? (978-1-60282-868-1)

Ghost Trio by Lillian Q. Irwin. When Lee Howe hears the voice of her dead lover singing to her, is it a hallucination, a ghost, or something more sinister? (978-1-60282-869-8)

The Princess Affair by Nell Stark. Rhodes Scholar Kerry Donovan arrives at Oxford ready to focus on her studies, but her life and her priorities are thrown into chaos when she catches the eye of Her Royal Highness Princess Sasha. (978-1-60282-858-2)

The Chase by Jesse J. Thoma. When Isabelle Rochat's life is threatened, she receives the unwelcome protection and attention of bounty hunter Holt Lasher who vows to keep Isabelle safe at all costs. (978-1-60282-859-9)

The Lone Hunt by L.L. Raand. In a world where humans and praeterns conspire for the ultimate power, violence is a way of life... and death. A Midnight Hunters novel. (978-1-60282-860-5)

The Supernatural Detective by Crin Claxton. Tony Carson sees dead people. With a drag queen for a spirit guide and a devastatingly attractive herbalist for a client, she's about to discover the spirit world can be a very dangerous world indeed. (978-1-60282-861-2)

Beloved Gomorrah by Justine Saracen. Undersea artists creating their own City on the Plain uncover the truth about Sodom and Gomorrah, whose "one righteous man" is a murderer, rapist, and conspirator in genocide. (978-1-60282-862-9)

Cut to the Chase by Lisa Girolami. Careful and methodical author Paige Randolph falls for brash and wild Hollywood actress, Avalon Randolph, but can these opposites find a happy middle ground in a town that never lives in the middle? (978-1-60282-783-7)

More Than Friends by Erin Dutton. Evelyn Fisher thinks she has the perfect role model for a long-term relationship, until her best friends, Kendall and Melanie, split up and all three women must reevaluate their lives and their relationships. (978-1-60282-784-4)

Every Second Counts by D. Jackson Leigh. Every second counts in Bridgette LeRoy's desperate mission to protect her heart and stop Marc Ryder's suicidal return to riding rodeo bulls. (978-1-60282-785-1)

Dirty Money by Ashley Bartlett. Vivian Cooper and Reese DiGiovanni just found out that falling in love is hard. It's even harder when you're running for your life. (978-1-60282-786-8)

Sea Glass Inn by Karis Walsh. When Melinda Andrews commissions a series of mosaics by Pamela Whitford for her new inn, she doesn't expect to be more captivated by the artist than by the paintings. (978-1-60282-771-4)

The Awakening: A Sisters of Spirits novel by Yvonne Heidt. Sunny Skye has interacted with spirits her entire life, but when she runs into Officer Jordan Lawson during a ghost investigation, she discovers more than just facts in a missing girl's cold case file. (978-1-60282-772-1)

Murphy's Law by Yolanda Wallace. No matter how high you climb, you can't escape your past. (978-1-60282-773-8)

Blacker Than Blue by Rebekah Weatherspoon. Threatened with losing her first love to a powerful demon, vampire Cleo Jones is willing to break the ultimate law of the undead to rebuild the family she has lost. (978-1-60282-774-5)

Another 365 Days by KE Payne. Clemmie Atkins is back, and her life is more complicated than ever! Still madly in love with her girlfriend, Clemmie suddenly finds her life turned upside down with distractions, confessions, and the return of a familiar face... (978-1-60282-775-2)

Silver Collar by Gill McKnight. Werewolf Luc Garoul is outlawed and out of control, but can her family track her down before a sinister predator gets there first? Fourth in the Garoul series. (978-1-60282-764-6)

The Dragon Tree Legacy by Ali Vali. For Aubrey Tarver time hasn't dulled the pain of losing her first love Wiley Gremillion, but she has to set that aside when her choices put her life and her family's lives in real danger. (978-1-60282-765-3)

The Midnight Room by Ronica Black. After a chance encounter with the mysterious and brooding Lillian Gray in the "midnight room" of The Griffin, a local lesbian bar, confident and gorgeous Audrey McCarthy learns that her bad-girl behavior isn't bulletproof. (978-1-60282-766-0)

Dirty Sex by Ashley Bartlett. Vivian Cooper and twins Reese and Ryan DiGiovanni stole a lot of money and the guy they took it from wants it back. Like now. (978-1-60282-767-7)

The Storm by Shelley Thrasher. Rural East Texas. 1918. War-weary Jaq Bergeron and marriage-scarred musician Molly Russell try to salvage love from the devastation of the war abroad and natural disasters at home. (978-1-60282-780-6)

Crossroads by Radclyffe. Dr. Hollis Monroe specializes in short-term relationships but when she meets pregnant mother-to-be Annie Colfax, fate brings them together at a crossroads that will change their lives forever. (978-1-60282-756-1)

Beyond Innocence by Carsen Taite. When a life is on the line, love has to wait. Doesn't it? (978-1-60282-757-8)

Heart Block by Melissa Brayden. Socialite Emory Owen and struggling single mom Sarah Matamoros are perfectly suited for each other but face a difficult time when trying to merge their contrasting worlds and the people in them. If love truly exists, can it find a way? (978-1-60282-758-5)

Pride and Joy by M.L. Rice. Perfect Bryce Montgomery is her parents' pride and joy, but when they discover that their daughter is a lesbian, her world changes forever. (978-1-60282-759-2)

Ladyfish by Andrea Bramhall. Finn's escape to the Florida Keys leads her straight into the arms of scuba diving instructor Oz as she fights for her freedom, their blossoming love…and her life! (978-1-60282-747-9)

Spanish Heart by Rachel Spangler. While on a mission to find herself in Spain, Ren Molson runs the risk of losing her heart to her tour guide, Lina Montero. (978-1-60282-748-6)

Love Match by Ali Vali. When Parker "Kong" King, the number one tennis player in the world, meets commercial pilot Captain Sydney Parish, sparks fly—but not from attraction. They have the summer to see if they have a love match. (978-1-60282-749-3)

One Touch by L.T. Marie. A romance writer and a travel agent come together at their high school reunion, only to find out that the memory of that one touch never fades. (978-1-60282-750-9)

The Raid by Lee Lynch. Before Stonewall, having a drink with friends or your girl could mean jail. Would these women and men still have family, a job, a place to live after…The Raid? (978-1-60282-753-0)

Month of Sundays by Yolanda Wallace. Love doesn't always happen overnight; sometimes it takes a month of Sundays. (978-1-60282-739-4)

Jacob's War by C.P. Rowlands. ATF Special Agent Allison Jacob's task force is in the middle of an all-out war, from the streets to the boardrooms of America. Small business owner Katie Blackburn is the latest victim who accidentally breaks it wide open, but she may break AJ's heart at the same time. (978-1-60282-740-0)

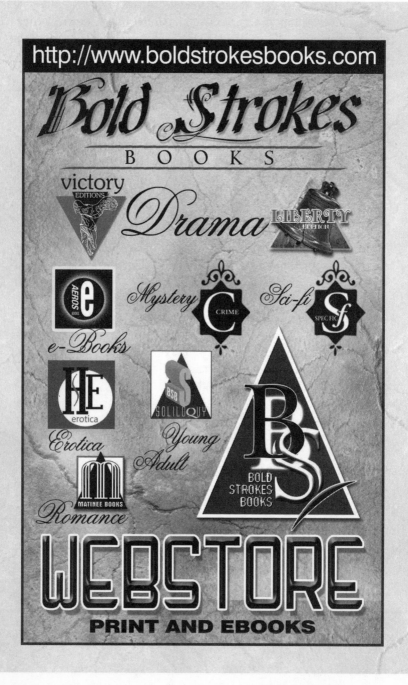